Mill

BEST SELLER ROMANCE

A chance to read and collect some of the best-loved novels from Mills & Boon—the world's largest publisher of romantic fiction.

Every month, two titles by favourite Mills & Boon authors will be republished in the *Best Seller Romance* series.

Sophie Weston

NO MAN'S POSSESSION

MILLS & BOON LIMITED
ETON HOUSE 18–24 PARADISE ROAD
RICHMOND SURREY TW9 ISR

First published in Great Britain 1984
by Mills & Boon Limited

Reprinted 1985
This edition 1992

ISBN 0 263 77622 0

Set in Monophoto Times 10 on 10½ pt.
02-9203-56159

Printed and bound in Great Britain

CHAPTER ONE

SUNLIGHT slanting in through the old sash windows turned the girl's auburn hair to burning copper. She did not look like an ordinary girl, excited because she had been offered an unusual assignment. Her face remained calm when she said, 'I'll do whatever he wants if the pay is good enough.'

Mrs Templeton was startled. More than that, she was horrified that Sara Thorn, who had always seemed such a good, quiet girl and an excellent worker, too, should say such a shocking thing. And without a blush.

'I don't think that's a nice way to talk, Sara, dear,' she said disapprovingly.

The girl shrugged thin shoulders. 'It's the truth,' she said in an unemotional voice.

The trouble was that Mrs Templeton believed her. In spite of her respectful manner and excellent work, there had always been something incalculable about Sara. Something, thought Mrs Templeton, who was not normally an imaginative woman, enigmatic. It was as if she was quiet and helpful because she had, for her own purposes, chosen to be; but if she decided to give free rein to her feelings, she would have been an altogether different person. Mrs Templeton gave herself a little shake. This fancifulness was unlike her and, anyway, was not getting the job done. She decided to ignore Sara's last remark.

'Professor Cavalli,' she said carefully, 'can be very—er—difficult to work for.'

And that, she thought, her lips tightening, was an understatement. They were all terrified of him, the girls she had sent round whenever he descended on Oxford and demanded instant, highly trained, secretarial service. Their skills had not been adequate to meet his requirements, their speeds had fallen short of the rate at which he wanted to work, and their nerves had frayed to pieces under his merciless tongue. And then, of course, the silly creatures compounded their errors by falling in love with him. For, when he was not dictating or shouting or cruelly mocking their shortcomings, Professor Cavalli had the charm of the devil and there was not one of Mrs Templeton's girls who had been proof against it.

Sara did not even ask how he was difficult. Mrs Templeton had the feeling that she did not greatly care.

She said, 'What does he want done?'

That was easy. Mrs Templeton said, 'Oh, it's usually papers he's given that he wants typed up for the printers. A few letters. Handouts for lectures, sometimes. He never does things till the last moment. He's always very busy.'

Sara appeared unmoved. Her ordinary job was a routine one but she had worked occasionally for temperamental academics before and they held no terrors for her. Indeed, though she could not of course tell Mrs Templeton so, nothing held any terrors for her any more. She felt as if she were frozen, untouchable by anxiety, moved only by one overwhelming determination. And even that, as she knew well enough, might be disappointed in the end. Even if she collected all the money she needed—and she was working all hours, typing theses at night and weekends to supplement her earnings—there was no guarantee that the operation would be successful.

'I'm not afraid of having to work under pressure,' she said now, to soothe Mrs Templeton's evident concern.

'No, I know.' The older woman got up and went to look out of her window into the street. In the May sunshine, the college buildings looked as if they had been constructed of butter and honey. It was one of Sara's major consolations, the serene beauty of Oxford's ancient buildings. Mrs Templeton, however, was not really seeing them.

'Sara, it wouldn't be fair if I didn't warn you—lots of the girls have worked for Professor Cavalli in the past and I couldn't ask any of them to do so again. I told Dr Fredericks last time it happened. I'd really prefer to say we have no one available this time but—well, Dr Fredericks knows that we're not particularly busy at the moment.'

And it was impossible to explain to the unworldly Dr Fredericks why she was reluctant to sacrifice the peace of mind of another of her secretaries to the whirlwind demands of Ben Cavalli.

'It's all right,' Sara said reassuringly. 'I can handle it.'

Mrs Templeton looked unhappy. 'I am sure you can handle the work, Sara. It's just Professor Cavalli. He can be very,' she hesitated, 'hurtful.'

Sara was faintly surprised. It was an odd thing to say, though some academics, she knew, could be very spiteful, though their spite was usually directed at colleagues and rivals rather than their secretaries. This Professor Cavalli must be quite spectacularly nasty. In the past she would have gone a long way to avoid someone like him. Nowadays she was harder.

'It won't upset me,' she told Mrs Templeton. 'I'm not easily hurt.'

Mrs Templton was troubled. 'You don't understand, Sara. You have no experience of Professor Cavalli. . . .'

'I have experience of plenty of home-grown temperaments, though,' Sara said wryly. 'All right, so he's Italian. It will all be a bit more operatic. I'm prepared for that.' She added with a flash of amusement, 'And for the money he's offering, I'd go and work for Baron Scarpia in person.'

That clinched it. Mrs Templeton came back to her

desk. She would tell Dr Fredericks that there was no one available. Sara Thorn had no idea of what was ahead of her or she would not be saying so blithely that the salary made it worthwhile. She might be avaricious, but she was young, younger than the other secretaries by five years and more, and Mrs Templeton was not going to take responsibility for exposing her to the likes of Ben Cavalli.

She said coldly, 'Money is not everything, Sara. It is time you learned that. I will have a word with Dr Fredericks and tell him that you might be available if Professor Cavalli insists. But I hope it will not come to that.'

It was dismissal. Sara rose composedly and left the supervisor's immaculate office. Nothing showed on her face, but underneath she was raging with disappointment. Cavalli was obviously a terror because the supplementary salary he was offering would virtually double her weekly wage. And if she had saved all of it, and worked for him for the three weeks Mrs Templeton thought he would be in Oxford, she might have been able to afford the operation a month earlier than the present timetable suggested. Damn Mrs Templeton and her kindly protectiveness, thought Sara with concentrated fury.

She went back to her desk and typed out schedules for the Inter Faculties Meeting with vicious speed and accuracy.

She walked home through the University Parks. It was a peaceful scene, cricket taking place in a leisurely fashion on one stretch of greensward, croquet further on, the little river murmuring, the trees in full leaf. The evening sun made a delicate tracery of shadow through the leaves and branches of a willow by the bank, and she paused. A punt glided past, silently except for the steady swish and fall of the punt pole in the hands of a young man. The passengers drowsed, unspeaking, in the sun. A profound loneliness struck Sara.

It was, she supposed, as well she was going to the party tonight. She did not really want to. When Chris had asked her she had not wanted to at all. But he had met her on the steps of the hospital after she had seen Mr Andrews. She must have looked shocked because he had swept her off to coffee and chatted to her laughingly about patients, some visiting specialist to whom he had been insufficiently respectful and the row he was conducting with his superior as a result, until she came back to normal.

She had not been able to bring herself to tell him what was wrong. But he had been so genuinely kind that when he asked her to accompany him to this evening's party, she had abandoned her usual practice and agreed. One evening away from the typewriter would make little difference, especially if the operation was so expensive that she would never be able to afford it anyway.

Sara walked on, aware that her ankle was stiffening. It did so every night. She told herself that the pain began at a later point every evening, that it was less intense than formally. But perhaps she was deceiving herself. She was desperate for signs of improvement and there had been so few in recent months. Mr Andrews' face had got longer and longer, though of course he had not told her to give up hope. And Sara herself was not going to surrender until she had proved to herself that she had done everything she could to get the ankle to take her weight again.

She had always had great determination. It was sheer willpower that had kept her at ballet classes in the first place. It had not been convenient for the orphanage. They had not impeded her, of course, because they were kindly people, but it was undeniable that they would have been very glad if little Sara Thorn's passion for ballet had worn off. But she had persisted and in the end had got her place in the London school of ballet.

It was willpower that had kept her there too. She was really too young to be on her own in London. She was, however, too old to attend some of the classes that she needed. Her training in Yorkshire had been good enough but old fashioned, and she had not danced every day as she should have done. If it had not been for the fierce determination that she had shown, those first months in London would have sent her exhausted and defeated back to the orphanage.

But she had worked. She had danced and practised and studied and exercised until ballet was her whole life. There had been no time for friends or parties or any of the other amusements that teenage girls usually enjoyed.

When she went to work for Sir Gerald, she had, if anything, worked even harder. But she had caught up now, she was no longer the awkward, half-trained schoolgirl. In the camaraderie of the *corps de ballet* she found friends. Her sense of fun, so long indulged only in private, won her affection. Her modesty, even when she began to dance solo while her companions remained consistently in the *corps de ballet*, ensured that she kept them. Sir Gerald, though distant, was benevolent. For the first time in her orphaned life she began to feel as if she belonged.

And then, of course, there had been Robert.

Sara was limping badly now, slowing down. She had left the Parks and was toiling up the paved sidewalk to her lodgings. Every step jarred and she felt the familiar shooting pain that seemed to explode from her ankle every third step. She put her head down and walked doggedly on.

She had loved Robert so much, been dazzled by him. He was already famous though not much older than herself; a brilliant young composer. Sara had been amazed that he was interested in her, astonished when he wanted her to marry him. Humbly, gratefully, she had agreed and, for a few months, life had been blissful.

He had seemed to adore her. They had so much in common. His parents had not liked her, of course, but he never seemed to let that make any difference. Sara, without family of her own, would have liked to love Robert's, but was not allowed to. She was not included in family gatherings, even when she and Robert were formally engaged, though his brother Michael's girlfriend, daughter of a Kensington neighbour, was always welcome.

The Ericssons thawed a little after Sara's first solo performance was received with acclaim. Robert had written a ballet for her then, 'The Shepherd and the Moon', and, after the first night, the papers had been full of the brilliance of their combined talents. Mrs Ericsson, almost cordial, had invited Sara on a shopping expedition and made her a present of a dress.

Sara knew quite well that it was because Mrs Ericsson did not think that anything in Sara's simple wardrobe was suitable for her son's fiancée to wear to the engagement party held by the family. But Sara was too happy and too much in love with Robert to quarrel with his mother over a silly thing like a dress. She had allowed her to choose it—a beautiful thing in wine velvet with old lace collar and cuffs—and had said 'thank you' prettily. In the end she had never worn it. Only two weeks later she had been in the accident which lamed her. The party was postponed while she was in hospital; then, when she came out, it was not discussed. Robert came to see her less and less. Eventually, Michael Ericsson had come, embarrassed, to say that Robert had been offered a teaching post in America and wanted to take it, but knew Sara was not strong enough to accompany him. Perhaps they could put the engagement into cold storage for a year while he went out there?

Hurt and furiously angry that Robert had sent his brother to parley with her, Sara had sat down and dashed off an impetuous letter, breaking the engagement. Robert had not come to see her in response. His mother did, however, to retrieve the engagement ring and bring a letter from Robert, full of half-promises for the future which Sara did not for a moment believe. A crippled wife would not suit Robert at all. He wanted her beautiful and famous and, if she was to be neither, he would find a replacement, she was sure. Bitterly hurt, she had torn the letter up in front of his mother.

'He's a weasel,' she had said coldly.

Mrs Ericsson had flushed. 'Try to see it from our point of view, Sara. We have to think of the future. . . .'

The future! It looked bleak enough to Sara. Lame, and likely to remain so, she was penniless and alone. More alone than she had ever felt in her life. Robert's defection had stabbed at the very heart of her existence. She had found somebody to whom she thought she was the most important person in the world, only to be proved wrong at the crucial time. For a while, she had not wanted to go on living.

Gradually, she had come out of her shell. Slowly she began to accept overtures of friendship from other people. Not much, and never for very long, but she found that she could now endure a little conversation, an occasional friendly cup of coffee, with other people without wanting to dissolve into tears.

And tonight she was going to a party.

It was being given by a fellow lodger, a leading light in the university orchestra. He was throwing it in honour of a visiting conductor after this evening's concert. Chris Franks had invited her to the concert as well, but she had declined. Music had a tendency to make her cry still; it was the only thing that did these days.

Sara turned into the gate, thankful to be home. Her

left leg was throbbing. She would need to rest it before the party. She hated the sensation of dragging the foot. It was so little that it was barely noticeable, but to Sara it was the height of ugliness. When she danced she had been beautiful. She was trained to it, and she had the instinct as well. Her every movement had been poetry. Now that it was all gone, she thought of herself as offensively unattractive.

She never gave a thought to her other attributes—a flawless skin, piquant, elfin face, great melting green eyes and hair like a fall of watered silk. She thought her fine-boned figure too thin and her whole appearance ordinary. She did not know that her delicate face with its hint of sadness had an appeal which meant that Chris Franks, saying that he was bringing her to the party, found himself the centre of a good deal of envy.

She dressed in her only suitable dress, the one Mrs Ericsson had given her. She had got over its associations and it made her look good. So good that Chris, arriving cheerfully to collect her, was taken aback.

'You're stunning.' He sounded a bit doubtful as if he wished she were less striking. 'When I asked you to the party I didn't know I'd have a film star on my hands.'

Sara gave him a warm smile. Even though she was sure it was flattery, his words gave her confidence. She had always been rather shy. Except when she was dancing, she liked to retire into the background. Parties such as the one she was about to enter had always been something of a trial. She slipped her hand into Chris's gratefully.

'How did your interview with the Old Man go?' she asked, remembering that he had foretold a telling off.

Chris looked wry. 'Not too bad considering. But I've got a penance—entertain the honoured guest while the Old Man goes off to a family dinner party. I collected him just before I came to get you.'

He opened the door into Mike's flat which was already half-full of people, most of whom Sara knew by sight. She accepted a glass of white wine and started talking to one of the geographers from downstairs. The girl's eyes registered surprise when she saw Sara.

'That's a gorgeous dress.'

'Gorgeous,' Sara agreed non-commitally, 'and very old.'

Her companion laughed. 'I wish my old clothes looked like that.'

Chris was clearly a sort of co-host. As soon as he was sure that Sara was happily talking to someone, he began to circulate with bottles, refilling glasses, replacing full ashtrays, stopping for a word here and there. Mike himself was nowhere to be seen.

'Mike's got to stand by while the visiting conductor has a drink with the Master, and then he's bringing him back here for the party. By the sound of it, a party is much more in his line than fraternising with the Senior Common Room,' Penny the geographer told her.

Sara glanced round idly. 'Do you know him, then?'

Penny shook her head. Her boyfriend played the violin in Mike's orchestra and she had heard a good deal about the demanding temperament of the guest conductor, she explained.

'They all seem to like him, though. Of course, he's very young in spite of being so famous.'

Sara was interested. Though she no longer went to concerts she still listened avidly to music on the radio. But Penny, whose main intererest in music was that her boyfriend, Oliver, played it, could not remember the name of the famous conductor.

The room was filling up now and people began to dance. The volume of noise increased as someone turned up the stereo and the guests began to talk in competition with it.

'I'd better get some of the food up from downstairs,'

Penny said, looking at her watch. 'There are trays of it in my room. Mike said I was to guard it with my life until he and the celebrity arrived, but I should think it will be all right to bring it up now. The concert should have finished twenty minutes ago.'

'I'll give you a hand,' offered Sara, and Penny thankfully accepted.

The stairs were dark and, though she negotiated the first journey easily enough in Penny's company, going down the second time for another tray, she tripped on a corner stair.

'Oh!' she exclaimed as her ankle turned and she lurched heavily sideways.

The sound sharpened into real fright as, instead of banging against the wall, she found herself caught hard and held against a strongly muscled chest.

'Oh, I'm sorry,' she apologised, flustered and off balance, her hands against a crisp shirt front, 'I didn't see you.'

There was a chuckle in answer. 'I didn't see you either,' a deep voice told her. It was slightly accented, and had a thread of distinct amusement running through it. 'I doubt if it would be possible to see the Taj Mahal in this light. Are you hurt?'

She drew back, wincing slightly as she put the damaged left foot to the floor. She took a limping step backwards.

'J-just startled,' she assured him untruthfully, detaching herself from the firm hands which had steadied her. 'I hope I didn't hurt you?'

'On the contrary, I could not have had a nicer welcome.' There was no doubt that he was laughing now. 'I was in two minds about coming to an undergraduate party, but I see I was wrong.'

It sounded as if this was the famous conductor, Sara thought. She was surprised that he was alone, as he seemed to be. She would have expected Mike to make a big entrance with his guest. Mike had a fondness for publicity. As a result, Sara had always been particularly wary of him.

She said coolly, 'If you're the guest of honour, shouldn't you be circulating?'

'Aha,' he said, as if at a pleasing discovery. 'You're the reception committee,' and reached for her again.

Sara flinched. There was a note in his voice which she had not heard for a long time. It was teasing, blatantly sensual. It said that he was intrigued and proposed to satisfy his curiosity. In her brief interlude of fame, a number of men had tried to flirt with her and she recognised the preliminaries.

'They'll be waiting for you,' she said, trying to make way for him to pass.

He ignored the movement. 'I doubt it. My host told me he was giving a party and I was welcome to come but I had the distinct impression he would just as soon I didn't.'

Sara frowned. *Not* Mike's conductor, by the sound of it.

'So, why did you come?' she asked, conscious that her tone was stiff. That flirtation with memory had recalled a lot of things she normally preferred to forget.

In the shadows, he shrugged. 'Impulse. I was at a loose end. I'm only in Oxford for one—er—performance,' the husky voice was full of self-mockery, 'and it didn't go too well. Curiosity. It's a long time since I was an undergraduate. I wanted to see what the young men get up to these days.' His voice warmed into laughter again, 'And I see it's not so different from when I was studying.'

So it had to be Mike's conductor. Sara found she did not like the implication of his words or the implied invitation of his tone. She drew back.

'As I said, I did not see you,' she said coldly, turning her shoulder to go past him.

'What ice!' he marvelled, refusing to budge. 'And to an honoured visitor, too.'

He shook his head mournfully. Sara could just see the movement in the dark. If this was Mark's guest conductor, she did not think much of him. She was seething. She took a step forward on to the half-landing.

'Will you let me pass?'

It brought her close up against his body. She was almost sure that he was shaking with silent laughter. He seemed determined to make a fool of her.

'If you pay toll,' he said, mock solemn.

In spite of the shadows, his hand found her chin with practised ease and turned her head towards him ... Sara was stiff with fury as his lips lightly brushed her own in a kiss that she was experienced enough to recognise was intended to tantalise.

He let her go.

'There. Toll paid. Not so dreadful, was it?'

'That,' said Sara between her teeth, 'depends on your point of view. *Now*, will you let me pass?'

There was a pause. Then he said very civilly, 'I'll do more than that. I'll give you safe conduct to the bottom of these very perilous stairs.' And before she knew what he was doing, he had lifted her off her feet and was running lightly down the flight. At the bottom, instead of setting her on her feet, he swung round and took her under the light in the hall before letting her go. Even then those iron hands rested on her shoulders lightly enough but, Sara was sure, well able to tighten if she were to try and make an escape. She was flustered and flushed. Normally a cool girl, she felt completely rocked off balance. She glared at him.

He looked back at her reflectively. He had clear blue eyes that just now were sparkling with merriment. At her expense, Sara thought furiously. He held her at arms' length and inspected her from top to toes with the air of a connoisseur. She could have hit him.

'Ah yes,' he said at length coolly, 'exquisite.' He touched her hair briefly. 'You look like one of those dear little devils from mediaeval paintings; all fire and flame and ferocity.'

Her eyes flashed and he caught the look and gave her a soft laugh.

'Well, little devil?'

Realising resignedly that it would be quite useless to struggle, Sara did her best to control her temper. He had the advantage, not only of strength, which was undoubted, but of initiative. Sara recognised that, if she threatened to scream her head off and make a fuss, this laughing-eyed stranger would see the ensuing scene as all part of the fun, whereas for Sara herself it would be humiliating.

She lowered her eyelids for a second and then said thoughtfully, 'I'm on my way to fetch food. If I don't return with it, a whole horde of hungry and vengeful devils will descend from Mike's room looking for sustenance. Do you want to be trampled to death in the rush?'

He shook his head, the blue eyes dancing. She gave him a sweet smile.

'Well then, wouldn't it be better if you let me go and deliver the rations?'

She did not make the mistake of trying to draw away before he let her. She stood calmly in the grip of his hands, her head slightly on one side, considering him. For a moment, his hand tightened and the blue eyes went dark. Then he let her go, laughing. Sara did her best to disguise her relief, turning away and going into Penny's room.

Coming out again with a tray, she found him still there, looking about him with that slight air of amusement which she had first noted. This was clearly a man who found the world an entertainment. Sara did not like him the better for making her feel a fool.

But she would not show her feelings. It was a point of pride not to let him suspect that she was wary of him. She held out the tray of little sandwiches and bridge rolls.

'Would you like something to eat? Are you hungry?'

He turned his head and looked at her, and that attractive lopsided smile grew. The blue eyes fixed themselves unmistakably on her mouth. To her annoyance, Sara felt a flush rising. He would see that too.

'Hungry?' he echoed, not taking his eyes from her lips. 'Just a little, but I can wait.'

She fled.

CHAPTER TWO

UPSTAIRS the party was in full swing now, in spite of the fact that neither the host nor the principal guest had yet appeared. Sara took her tray of nibbles round the room from people in animated groups to couples interested only in each other. Dancing had started, and the music was loud.

She met Chris a couple of times circulating with big bottles of cheap wine. He grimaced at her.

'Complete monkey house, isn't it? Mike must have asked the whole college.'

Sara nodded smiling, but did not attempt to answer. She judged it would put too great a strain on her voice.

'Dance with me later,' Chris urged, 'when I've emptied a couple more bottles.'

She hesitated for the briefest moment. Dancing of any kind, even bopping around on Mike's threadbare carpet, would put a strain on the ankle which was already beginning to ache a little. But then, why try to avoid strain? Since there might be nothing that she could afford to have done about it, she might as well learn to live with it. And she certainly could not spend the rest of her life refusing to dance with pleasant young men in the remote hope that by conserving her energy she might somehow return to her shattered career. She nodded agreement and Chris, not noticing the shadow in her eyes, moved on, well satisfied.

The next time she saw him he was talking to the man she had met on the stairs. Sara stopped dead, aware of a slight prickle in her spine. She did not want to meet that man again, even in the protective company of Chris. But she could not take her eyes off him.

In the dim light of the hallway, she had got no more than the vaguest impression of height and darkness. Now she could see him clearly. There was, she thought wryly, every reason for that devastating confidence. He was quite simply one of the most handsome men she had ever seen. He was tall, of course, taller than Chris by more than a head; in that, she had not been mistaken. He was also very dark, the hair that curled on to his collar in stark contrast to the white material. In profile, he looked remote, formidable but, when he turned, as he did now, she looked straight into dancing blue eyes. She saw him lift his glass in silent toast and, blushing, fled back downstairs to replenish her tray.

Mike was arriving. There was a commotion on the stairs that announced his party. Sara drew back warily into the lea of Penny's door.

She quite liked Mike, but he was fond of publicity. If he found that little Sara Thorn on the top floor was the brilliant Sara Romana who had so mysteriously disappeared from the ballet scene after one widely acclaimed season, he would not be above informing the press of the fact.

She gave them time to arrive, be greeted and start to mingle, and then she followed him with the last plates of food. She paused in the doorway, noting with amusement that someone had dimmed the lights. It could not be Chris. Chris was still something of a schoolboy, unlike Mike who shared with his alarming guest of honour a notable sophistication.

Mike, she saw, was not with his guest but, instead, was talking animatedly to a group of musicians, some of whom she knew by sight. One, in particular, was familiar. He turned his head a little in conversation, and she froze.

Robert Ericsson. Robert *here*! Sara felt as if her blood had turned to water. He was in America, she was sure of it. What was he doing in Oxford? The new composition they had been playing tonight—could it have been Robert's? Why, oh, why had she not thought to ask?

But now she must get out and fast. She moved to the door and was brought up short by a touch on her elbow.

'Found!' said her captor mockingly. 'I claim my prize of a dance.' And as she stared at him, shaking, 'You must have known I'd find you again.'

Sara shook her head numbly.

'You shouldn't wear such an incendiary dress if you want to go unnoticed,' he said hardly. 'A flame in the darkness would be less obtrusive. Come and dance.'

She shook her head. 'N-no, thank you, I— It's too late. I have to work tomorrow.'

He gave a soft laugh. 'I won't get you to bed too late,' he promised, putting a hand under her elbow. 'But first come and dance.'

She would have resisted. She was already pulling against that hard grip when she saw Robert staring at her. He was looking as if he could not believe his eyes. Sara lifted her chin and outstared him. He looked sad, pitying. She flinched. She could not take pity, least of all from Robert. She turned to her companion with a brilliant, blind smile.

'All right. One dance, and then I must go.'

He looked at her thoughtfully. Afterwards she realised that he must have followed the direction of her gaze and seen Robert looking at them. At the time, she knew nothing except that she wanted to lose herself in the crowd where Robert could not find her.

They danced well together. Or rather, they would have done if she had not been stiff with reaction. He had a natural sense of rhythm. His arms went round her smoothly, as if they had been dancing together for years. The music was slow, insidious. A husky voice was whispering into a microphone about the sorrows of lost love. Sara felt her throat tighten, though she knew it was ridiculous. It must be the cheap wine she had drunk.

She felt she was floating, hardly aware of her partner. Her head dropped against his shoulder and she thought she heard him murmur into her hair. She did not know what he said; it sounded as if it were in a foreign tongue. She turned her head slowly against his shirt, and looked up at him.

The eyes, intensely blue, burned down into her own. A small smile was curling the fine mouth.

'Yes?' he said, as if she had asked him something.

She was light-headed and bewildered. He ran his hands up her yielding spine.

'Come along, I'll take you home.'

She stared. 'But I only live upstairs. In the top flat.'

His mouth quirked. 'Then I'll see you upstairs.'

She did not query his decision. She was tired, drained. She did not want an argument. And besides, if she walked out of the party in the company of this stranger, there would be an excellent reason for Robert not to follow her. She lowered her eyes so as not to look at Robert.

The stairs were lit, dimly but adequately, by the light from Mike's room. When they reached Sara's room, it was not in darkness either. She must have forgotten to switch off her reading lamp. It lit the rug and armchair in a little pool of warmth. Outside, it was now black night. The stars were out and the branch of the sycamore that brushed against her window was a twisted shape masking the moon.

He looked about him, standing in the doorway.

'You live here? All the time? Or do you go home during the vacations?'

Sara shook her head, swallowing. There had never been a home to go to, but nobody knew that.

'No, I live here permanently.'

He strolled forward, glancing at the sloping ceiling. 'Very cosy, under the eaves. Do you like old places?'

She thought about it. 'I've never considered. Yes, I suppose I do. I've always lived in old places anyway. But then, I could live anywhere, I think.'

'Could you?'

She sat down in the armchair and now he came and dropped to his knees in front of her, turning her chin so that her face was brought into the play of the light.

'Could you, indeed? And yet, you look such a fastidious little thing.'

She was surprised again. He was a very disconcerting man, with those laughing eyes that sometimes did not laugh at all but looked as if they had penetrated your most private thoughts and his odd, intimate remarks. She frowned.

'Don't look so worried.' He put his finger on her forehead, smoothing out the lines. 'Why are you so tense? Don't you trust me?'

'I don't know you,' she pointed out, drawing back.

'No, you don't do you?' he said with an odd inflection in his voice. 'You haven't even asked my name.' He paused, and when she said nothing, he added in a caressing undertone, 'Sara.'

She jumped, startled and a little afraid. It seemed that, in discovering her name, he had taken possession of some part of her without her being aware of it. Her eyes flew to his.

'I asked,' he said in a different tone, amused again, 'I wanted to know. I want to know everything about you.'

She shrank even more. She knew nothing about flirting, although it was a game she had seen friends play often enough. But she had worked too hard, been too occupied. She had watched and wondered, and sometimes been a little wistful, but she had never done it herself. Stopping it before it started. Now she was alarmed. Did this man think she was practised in the art of flirtation as he clearly was himself? She was older than the undergraduates at the party. Did he think that meant that she was more experienced than they were also? If he did, he was painfully wrong.

She croaked, 'Why?' half afraid of the answer, but unable to keep back the question.

His expression was wry. 'You're a contradiction. I like contradictions, puzzles. I want to know why a girl who looks like a living flame behaves like a Victorian schoolgirl. At least, some of the time,' he amended, his eyes on her lips.

Sara was mesmerised as he drew nearer. Normally, she was shy, slightly withdrawn. This evening, because of the wine she had drunk or because of the shock of seeing Robert, she felt different, reckless. She looked at that firm mouth, the eyes whose laughter did not disguise the fact that they were intent. Sara trembled, but, for the first time in her life, did not draw away.

He put out a gentle hand, touched her lower lip with a finger tip. She gasped at the sensation it aroused and his eyes darkened. His other hand slid round her and drew her body towards his own. She went, unresisting.

'You look as if you're in a dream,' he told her softly, that note of laughter still there.

His long fingers were moving at the back of her neck, tantalising her at the same time as they soothed. Sara began to realise that she was in the hands of an expert. Her lips parted and her head fell back against his shoulder. For just a moment, he was still, looking down at her, the eyes almost black and the mouth a firm, straight line, all laughter banished. Then he lowered his head.

It was as if she had never been kissed before. The touch of his mouth was like putting a match to a powder keg. Sara was instantly on fire, giving back kiss for kiss with an intensity she had never imagined. She felt engulfed, consumed, helpless in the flame he had ignited. When his mouth left hers, she clung to him trembling.

He moved, transferring the weight of their bodies neatly so that he drew her down beside him on the rug before she realised what he was about. He took her face between his hands and stared at her for a long moment, smiling.

'Very rewarding,' he drawled.

Sara blushed and lowered her eyes. She knew what she must look like, after her brush with unaccustomed passion. She put a hand to smooth her tousled hair and he caught it and carried it to his lips.

'No, don't tidy yourself. You look very sweet, all rosy and rumpled.'

Sara could feel herself blushing harder. But she did not take her hand away and, when he turned it over and brushed a kiss across the soft palm, she could not have prevented her little shiver of pleasure to save her life.

He gave a soft sound of pure satisfaction, pushing her gently till she lay full length. He kissed her again, almost tentatively at first, as if he sensed her doubts and was determined to soothe them away. It was that skilful tenderness which was Sara's final undoing. Her shy hesitation left her. She reached for him, running her fingers through the springy hair, along the hard muscled body, as if she had been making love to him all her life.

He found the small velvet-covered buttons that did up the front of her dress and dealt with them expertly, drawing the material away from her body with the utmost care, sliding the sleeves down her arms to the wrists until at last, she lay exposed to his gaze. He propped himself up on an elbow beside her. In an agony of shyness, Sara's eyelashes fluttered down.

'Why do you do that?' asked the low voice in her ear. 'Don't you like me to look at you?'

She shook her head, not answering.

'Then why?'

He stroked the back of his hand very lightly across her breast. Sara felt her whole body quicken and had to bite her lip to stop herself crying out.

'Do you think I'll hurt you?' went on that soft, implacable voice.

Again, she shook her head, screwing up her eyes like a child.

'Sara, look at me.' It was a command. 'We won't do anything you don't want.'

Ah, but there was nothing she did not want to do with him except let him go. She had never felt like this before; had no experience on which to call. She had been wholly his from that first devastating kiss, and now there was no way to hide the fact. She turned her head away.

She knew with absolute certainty that Robert had never made her feel like this. She had loved him, felt safe with him, wanted above everything else to be his wife. But she had never craved for his touch as she did now for this man.

It was a shattering revelation of her own nature. She felt frightened. It was as if, simply by touching her, this man had put a spell on her so that she was no longer what she had been before but something else that he chose. Sara had never before felt so wholly in the power of someone else. Nor such a stranger to herself.

'Oh, Sara, *Sara*,' he said against her skin.

And she was not proof against that husky pleading note. Her lashes lifted. Silently, their eyes met. Sara's were brilliant with desire, very green, half-ashamed, half-puzzled. He drew a long breath.

Still holding her eyes with his own, his hand began to explore her soft body. At her breast, it lingered and Sara tensed, her lips parting in a soundless gasp. He smiled, kissed her mouth gently and then, so lightly that it was almost an agony, his lips began to travel the same path as his hand.

Sara could bear it no longer. Her body arched towards him in inarticulate surrender. Half-drowned in desire, she had no clear idea of how he freed her from the rest of her clothes, nor where he disposed of his own. All she knew was that she wanted, needed to be close to him, closer than naked skin against skin and that she was moving against him in a frenzy of need.

He seemed startled, almost amused. Though no less aroused than she, he was more in command of himself, of both of them. He lifted himself away from her and caressed her tautening body until Sara could no longer repress a groan, her eyes, her whole body, begging for fulfilment.

It was then that she became aware of a commotion outside. Earlier there had been voices, feet on the stairs which she had registered dimly but which had not intruded on her consciousness. Now there was a thundering at the door. Someone was battering his fist on it, over and over again, calling her name. Shaking with passion as she was, it took her a moment to register what was happening.

'Sara. I know you're in there. Don't be a child. I want to talk to you.'

She stiffened slightly.

'Open this door!'

She could not bear it. She clung with all her might to the moment, to the dark, bewildering circle of pleasure and pain that surrounded her. She would not listen to the intruders.

Sara turned her mouth to his and kissed him hard, with a kind of desperation, as the knocking recommenced accompanied by that slurred, demanding voice.

It was Robert. Even though she had not heard his voice for more than twelve months, she recognised him. She winced.

'Sara, do you hear me?'

'Who is he?' demanded the man who was holding

her, not bothering to lower his voice. Suddenly, he sounded cool and alarmingly in control of himself. Sara, who was still shaking, could not help being chilled. 'A discarded suitor?'

'N-no. Not quite.'

The dark blue eyes narrowed. 'Not quite discarded? I don't think I follow. What right has he to come up here at this time of night and hammer on your door?'

Sara closed her eyes, fighting for self-control. 'He's my fiancé,' she managed at last.

'What?'

He looked astounded and, for a moment, his eyes were molten with fury, then his face changed, rearranged itself into an expression of faint boredom. He reached behind him for his shirt.

'Then I must obviously be going,' he said with cool politeness, pulling the shirt over his head.

Sara was horrified at the effect of her words. She should have explained that the engagement was over, had been over at Robert's request for more than a year. She opened her mouth but, in her agitation, the words that came out only made things worse.

'Oh no, please, you mustn't think . . . I mean, don't go because Robert. . . .'

He was standing, pulling on his clothes, looking down at her with a faint, insolent smile.

'You're very flattering, but I think it would be better. I had not realised you were another's man's possession.'

Sara's head reared back. She met his angry eyes straight on.

'I'm no man's possession,' she said between her teeth.

He gave a soft laugh, letting his eyes wander down her nakedness in a pantomime of appreciation which brought the blood to her cheeks and had her fumbling for something to cover herself. His mouth moved in a mocking smile.

'That would be a pity,' he told her.

There was a shawl draped over the threadbare seat of the armchair and she dragged that round herself, shivering. In the distance, Robert could be heard clattering downstairs complaining to someone. Presumably Mike or one of the others had come up to get him and lead him away. They would all think it was a good joke, Robert hammering on her door in the middle of the night. She wondered whether he had told them why, whether they knew now what she had been to Robert and, more important, who she had been before the accident. Perhaps they had put it all down to drink. It was obvious that he had had too much, his slurred voice had given him away.

She hugged the shawl round her, shaking convulsively, not able to look at the man who stood there despising her. She had never felt so vulnerable in her life. She could only pray that he would go and she need never see him again.

He moved, bent to her, and took one slender hand away from her shoulder to which she was clinging and raised it to his lips in a parody of courtesy.

'A great pity,' he repeated, lightly, insultingly. 'You're a passionate little creature.' He took her chin in his hand and turned her unwilling face up to him. 'Your fiancé could be a lucky man. If he didn't make you wait too long, that is. Was that what this evening was about? Were you punishing him?'

The green eyes darkened as if he had hit her. Sara said nothing, folding her lips together to stifle a protest. If that was what he wanted to think, it made no difference. She would have made love to him tonight, without hesitation or reservations, while he, as was obvious from the speed with which he had collected himself, had been playing a game.

She said at last, in a low voice, as if she had not heard his last insult, 'Would you please go now? Goodnight.'

For a moment, his fingers tightened cruelly on her jaw. The pain brought tears to her eyes, but she was too proud to cry before him. If once she started to let the tears fall, she knew it would be a long time before they stopped.

'Goodnight,' she repeated steadily.

At that, he gave a harsh laugh and almost flung her away from him. She caught at the shawl. Her hand was shaking, she noticed with detached interest, and clenched almost convulsively on the shawl. She sank back among the cushions, feeling drained. She, who never made an ungraceful movement in her life, huddled in an ugly crouch, clutching the shawl around her.

Sara moistened her lips. She felt bewildered, dazed with pain. Her body had ceased to obey her and she did not know what was happening. She felt shipwrecked. Her body was an undisciplined stranger, responding to this man as if it were an instrument that he alone knew how to make music on.

She had loved Robert, cried for him when he deserted her. But tonight she had first run away from him and then, when he had pursued her, she had blocked her ears and tried instead to drown herself in unaccustomed passion. Passion, moreover, in a stranger's arms.

She passed a shaking hand over her eyes. 'Goodnight,' she said for the third time.

She could not look at him. There was a pause.

Then—'Goodbye,' he said coolly, as if he were correcting her.

She heard the door close.

For a long time, she did not move. Her throat ached but she found she could not cry. She felt hurt as she had not felt since Robert had broken their engagement, but she did not know why. Bewildered, she knuckled her eyes and then stopped. She realised, with a little shock of dismay, that she had never even asked his name.

It would be better that way, she told herself,

staggering a little as she got to her feet. She would never see him again, she devoutly hoped, and she would not even have a name to try to forget. It would make it easier to put the whole of this evening's events out of her mind. She looked wryly at the hand that still trembled—but would it be so easy to put it out of her body?

She turned her back on the thought then and later. She had used work as a therapy before and, the next day, she threw herself into her allotted tasks, working at lightning speed, accurate to the last comma. At noon, to her surprise, the Head of Registry, Dr Fredericks, asked to see her.

Sara knocked on his door, and, receiving no answer, went in. Dr Fredericks was kneeling on the carpet looking at a street map before him. Sara could see that it was old. She walked round it carefully and coughed. Dr Fredericks leaped to his feet.

'Oh, yes. Good morning Miss Er—um. I was just looking at this map. Excellent condition. Now, what was it that I wanted to see you about—they didn't tell you?' he asked Sara, with a gleam of hope. When she shook her head, he murmured, 'No, they never do anything useful. Well, I shall have to put my mind to it.'

In spite of Sara's overwhelming feeling of shamed misery, she could not help being entertained by Dr Fredericks' aid to memory. He darted to his desk, flung himself back in an enormous chair which he sent swivelling energetically, and muttered.

'I was *here* when Janet brought in the post.' He slapped a hand on the wire basket, and papers fell to the floor. Sara restored them. 'Then Hill rang,' he picked up the telephone receiver and put it down again, 'and Ben Cavalli brought me the Tadussi map and told me he'd found the girl he wanted. . . .' He broke off, and an extraordinary convulsion seemed to have come over his kindly face. He ran his glasses up and down his nose several times in agitation. 'That is, he *must* have a secretary to go with him to Venice at once. And they tell me you're willing,' he ended on a rush, like a child coming to the end of a recitation. 'So you must go and see him at once, please, Mrs Templeton will give you the details. At once.'

And he hustled her out of the door as if he did not dare to give her the opportunity to open her mouth. Sara, bewildered, left.

Mrs Templeton was not free until the next day. Sara mulling over the oddity of the offer and Dr Fredericks' manner, decided that it was all due to the elderly don's eccentricity. She would have been glad to discuss it with somebody but there was nobody in the house to whom she was close enough.

Chris was wholly taken up with his own affairs. He did not even ask about her early departure from the party or the scene that Robert had made afterwards.

'I spent all my time butlering,' he told her gloomily.

She laughed, beginning to feel more comfortable. In the face of such indifference, her embarrassment subsided.

When Mike came in, it was different. He looked at her beadily. Fortunately, by that time, she had regained her self-possession and looked back calmly enough.

'I didn't know you knew Ericsson,' he said, helping himself to cold meat and sitting down beside her at the scrubbed pine table. 'Known him long?'

'I haven't seen him for ages,' Sara said evasively, buttering bread with energy.

'No, so he said. Didn't seem to expect to see you in Oxford,' Mike persisted.

'No?'

'He seemed to think you were avoiding him. Got very—er—annoyed about it,' Mike told her tantalisingly.

She refused to show interest. Mike must have realised that Robert was very drunk by the end of the party when he went in search of her. She was not going to feed his curiosity.

'Really?' she said in a colourless voice.

Mike gave up. 'Well, he won't have any trouble in tracking you down again. He's in Oxford for a couple of days and then comes back next week for the rest of the term. He's exchanging with Duncan, he tells me,' Mike announced to the table at large, disappointed with her reaction.

Chris was interested and asked where the tutor in music was going, and what he was going to do. Against the background of casual conversation, Sara sat as if turned to stone. It was not true; it could not be true. Robert had the job in America. He would not be able to abandon it so lightly, surely?

But something told her that it was all too horribly true. Her sanctuary had been discovered and, if Mike was right, was likely to be invaded. Sara began to crumble bread blindly, kneading the crumbs with fingertips that shook.

She had little doubt that Robert would seek her out. He had proved that the other night. Besides—she bit her lip. He wanted her. He had always wanted her but she had been timorous and very shy, in spite of their engagement. She had held him off and sometimes it had exasperated him. But in the end he had always laughed and let her have her way, saying tenderly that she would change in time.

And now, she had changed. Staring into the middle distance, unaware of her companions and their conversation, Sara recognised the bitter fact that she had changed beyond recognition.

It had not been Robert who had taken her over the threshold into the knowledge of her body's imperatives. But whoever had been her guide, she knew herself now and could not go back to her former innocence. If Robert wanted her now and chose to exert himself, would she still, for all her pride and last time's hurt, be able to refuse him?

She must get away, leave Oxford, flee the advancing threat before she found out the answer. Sara was almost certain that she could not bear to see him again. But if she did—she had no idea whether or not she would fall into his arms. She no longer knew what she might be capable of in the way of folly. She must not find out.

The job in Italy suddenly became not just desirable; it was essential.

Mrs Templeton called her to her office first thing the next day. Dr Fredericks had gone against her advice and she was not pleased. Mind you, the girl deserved it with that foolhardy claim that she would do anything for enough money. But, all the same, Mrs Templeton felt that punishment by Professor Cavalli was too extreme.

She said, pityingly, 'If you've changed your mind, you don't have to go, you know, Sara. Nobody will hold it against you. Dr Fredericks likes to oblige Professor Cavalli if he can, but he's under no obligation to him.'

The green eyes, dark today so that they were almost the grey of storm clouds, looked at her blankly. She had the feeling that Sara Thorn's thoughts were far away in no very pleasant place.

'I would like to go to Italy,' Sara said pleasantly, like a well-mannered automaton.

'It may be at very short notice.'

Sara gave a little shiver, thinking of Robert's impending arrival.

'The sooner, the better.'

Mrs Templeton looked concerned. 'My dear, forgive me for mentioning it, but are you in some kind of trouble? Is there anything I can do?'

The long lashes quivered and then lifted. Sara looked

at her as if she were seeing her for the first time. A faint, haunted smile touched the delicate mouth.

'Thank you, but no. There isn't anything anyone can do,' Sara said desolately.

And that, at least, she thought, was the truth. She was a walking disaster area. Her injured ankle seemed to hurt all the time now, without respite, and her heart did not seem to be in much better condition. She was in a constant state of near panic. Every time she went round a corner, she braced herself in case she bumped into Robert. Robert or—she quashed the thought before it formed. Robert, her career, even her own wanton behaviour she could not bear to think of. The man who had set fire to her defences and dragged into the light needs within herself which she had not previously suspected, him she could not bear to remember. She was rigid with the effort of not remembering.

Mrs Templeton gave up.

'He's at the Boar's Head,' she said. 'You'd better go and see him now. He's expecting you.'

Like a well-programmed robot, Sara went. At the hotel she was immediately taken up to the professor's suite on the first floor. Following a pageboy, Sara marvelled distantly at her own lack of nerves. Normally, she would have been apprehensive at an interview for a job, especially one in which she had received such comprehensive advance warning about the interviewer. But she was so worn down with the events of the last two days that she was quite calm.

The pageboy knocked and was told to enter. He held the door open for Sara to pass in front of him, and she went into the room, thanking the boy with a smile.

It was a comfortably furnished sitting room with a large mirror over a stone fireplace. A man was standing in front of the unlit fire, one foot on the polished brass fender, a couple of sheets of paper in one hand, a cigarettte hanging negligently from the other. He was reading and did not turn immediately. Sara looked at the back of that bent head and felt a faint stirring of recognition.

It turned into a full-scale flare of alarm as he raised his head and deep blue eyes met hers in the mirror. His smile was mocking and unforgettable. Sara's heart sank like a stone.

He swung neatly on his heel and came towards her.

CHAPTER THREE

'THANK you,' he said to the boy.

Sara was rooted to the spot. There was a clinking as some coins changed hands, and then the boy left with his tip. It must have been a large one because he had a great grin on his face. Sara thought that she did not like the knowing look in her direction which accompanied it.

The professor closed the door behind the pageboy, and then leaned his shoulders against its solid panels. He did not, Sara decided, still in her state of cold shock, look like a professor of anything. In fact, barring the exit and eyeing her with a distinctly challenging gleam in those startling eyes, he resembled nothing so much as an old-style gangster. She pondered over telling him so and decided against it. There was no point in offering him more reasons for disliking her.

She said instead, 'What are you doing here?'

The smile grew. Sara saw it and was not reassured.

'Waiting to interview you,' he said literally. 'I gather you're prepared to come to Venice and do my typing. In fact, I am told you're prepared to do a good deal more than that if asked. Anything for money, they told me.' He shook his head in a pantomime of disapproval 'Shocking, these modern girls.'

'It's not like that,' Sara began hotly.

The eyes glinted. 'No?' The voice was soft, idle; you would have thought he was not particularly interested in the subject. 'Then tell me what it is like.'

Sara bit her lip. She was not fooled by the languid pose. Under the lazy eyelids his glance was keen. She had already nearly betrayed herself. In self-defence she had nearly poured out the whole story of her injury and the operation she needed. But if she told him that, she was nearly certain that he would not be satisfied. He would want to know it all. And she did not have the courage to tell anyone the whole story.

She made a little helpless gesture. 'I need a job, that's all.'

She glared at him, suddenly defiant. This seemed only to amuse him. The bright blue eyes locked with hers and she almost rocked under the impact. For a long moment, she withstood the blaze of his eyes. She lifted her chin and he turned away abruptly.

'You're a liar,' he said with great calm. 'That is far from all. But I shall find out eventually. You will tell me.'

Sara drew a long, steadying breath. She felt as if she had been running into a high wind and the relief that he was not pursuing the subject further was enormous. She judged it better not to reply to his last remark which was clearly designed to provoke her. He must have realised that, when she was angry, she forgot to guard her tongue. If he wanted to find out her secrets, he must have deduced that he needed first to get her off her guard. Sara frowned, puzzled and faintly alarmed.

'Who are you?' she demanded.

'Ah.' He stubbed out the cigarette very carefully and folded the papers in his hand. 'It's taken you a long time to ask that.' He paused. 'Although you already know the answer. You have a letter in your bag addressed to me, I believe.'

Sara brushed that aside impatiently. 'I know your name is Cavalli. But why are you interested in my affairs? What possible concern can it be of yours why I want the job you are offering? As long as I am competent to do it, of course.'

'Of course,' he agreed politely. Too politely, she suddenly realised, as he went on in that soft voice, 'My name is Cavalli, and I am your prospective employer and that is all you want to know about me. You are dangerously incurious, my dear, since you contemplate spending the next six months in my company in my country.'

Sara stared. 'Are you warning me not to take the job?' she asked in genuine bewilderment.

The smile twisted. 'I am warning you not to keep your eyes shut, Sara Thorn. You may walk into more than you bargained for.'

She said wryly, 'I think I already have.'

A startled look crossed his face, quickly banished. He surveyed her with evident appreciation.

'Well, thank God for that, at least.'

He flung himself down in a wing chair and gestured her to another. She hesitated but eventually sat on the edge of the seat, her hands clasped on her clutch bag. It helped to still their trembling.

Sara was furious with herself. There was no reason why she should be afraid of this man. It had been a nasty little scene with him after the party, true, but that was no justification for her sitting trembling before him like a naughty schoolgirl. There were other jobs.

She said with undisguised hostility, 'So what is it that you want me to do in Venice? *If* I take the job.'

His eyes mocked her and she found herself blushing. It did nothing to sweeten her temper.

'The *job*,' he said with wicked amusement, 'is a very simple one of typing a thesis. What else I may want you to do,' he gave a little shrug, 'we will leave for discussion at the time.'

Sara gasped at the insolence. 'A thesis?' she queried, as coolly as she could manage. To her own ears she sounded positively disdainful. 'Isn't that a little superfluous if you are already a professor?'

He was laughing openly. 'Oh, I can assure you that I am a proper professor, *cara*. I have any number of ornate certificates conferring degrees on me by a number of universities. But if you are worried you can always check my credentials in the university handbooks.'

Sara gave him a sweet smile, 'I shall, of course, do so.'

'Naturally.' The wretched man gave every sign of enjoying himself hugely. 'No, the thesis is not mine, as you rightly supposed. It is the work of my Uncle Luigi. He is the adventurous member of the family and, in his young days, was a great traveller. Then he fell ill and could do nothing. When he began to get better I—it was suggested that he should study. He ran away from home before completing his formal education, you understand. And then—since my family possesses a noted collection of ancient maps—he determined to write a book about them. It should earn him his doctorate, for which he is most anxious. It will also serve as a guide to the collection.'

Sara nodded her head. It was the sort of assignment she had had before, and she had little doubt that she could manage it. But why could the manuscript not be sent to her? It suited her well enough to leave Oxford for the time being, but she could not understand why it should suit Professor Cavalli. It would be so much less expensive simply to send the manuscript to the typist.

'Why do I have to go to Venice to type it?' she asked bluntly.

His eyes narrowed. 'Does he not want you to go then?'

She was confused. 'He? Who?'

He made a contemptuous gesture, flicking his fingers as if dismissing some lap dog.

'The—er—noisy fiancé who interrupted us the other evening.'

Sara went scarlet. He surveyed her flaming cheeks with interest.

'Charming,' he said in a tone which suggested he was

applauding a performance. 'There are so few girls who blush these days.'

She was indignant but was too embarrassed to protest.

'I can understand his disliking the idea,' he went on lightly, 'but I'm afraid he will have to put up with it. If you want the job, of course. And I am told you do.'

She could do nothing but nod her head mutely.

'Then, as far as I'm concerned, it is settled. Though you have not even asked about the salary, and it may not suit you.'

He named a sum which, to Sara's distracted mind, seemed enormous.

'And, of course, your fare and your accommodation in Venice will be taken care of. And now, if you will forgive me,' he looked at his watch, 'I have another appointment. If you will leave me your references, I will just confirm them, though I am sure my uncle will be happy to have your services. The Registry speak highly of you.'

She handed over the envelope with which she had come prepared.

'When——' her voice rasped, and she had to clear her throat and start again, 'when do you want me to go to Venice? I shall have to hand in my notice.'

'Do so at once,' he instructed.

She raised her eyebrows at his tone. He gave her a sudden and devastating grin.

'No, that was a bit high-handed, wasn't it? What I meant was, tell them you've agreed to come with me. I'll see old Fredericks and ask him to release you when I need you. He'll tell me if it isn't convenient.'

Sara tried to imagine the mild Dr Fredericks saying 'no' to this man, and failed. Seeing her expression, he laughed softly.

'I assure you he will. And I shall accommodate him.'

'And *my* convenience?' Sara enquired.

He looked bored. 'My dear girl, you're being paid—and exceptionally well, as you must realise—to fit in. I'm afraid your convenience is irrelevant. Start your packing now, and be ready to leave when I say.'

Sara had a feeling she was being deliberately baited. So she held on to her temper saying in her most remote voice, 'Then I shall have to leave you my address so that you can get in touch with me quickly.'

The blue eyes glinted.

'I remember very well where you live,' he told her, 'exactly.'

This time she did not blush. 'How fortunate. Then I need waste no more of your time.'

She rose gracefully and went to the door. He followed her as if to shake hands but, instead of her right, he took her left in both of his and turned it over, scrutinising. It was bare of rings. There was no longer even the mark of untanned skin which had for a time borne silent witness to her broken engagement.

'I see you do not wear his ring, even when you are not at parties,' he said blandly. 'How wise.'

She tried to ease out of his clasp, but it was firm. He took her hand to his lips in a parody of courtesy and just touched his mouth against the whitened knuckles. Sara jumped as if she had been burned by the touch. He chuckled.

'One great advantage of Venice,' he promised kindly, 'no intrusive fiancés.'

It was only afterwards that Sara realised that he had not asked any of the questions which he should have done and for which she had been prepared. She tried to find out what he had already been told about her work and drew a blank. It had all been agreed between him and Dr Fredericks she was told. Mrs Templeton knew nothing about it. Sara began to suspect that the interview had been irrelevant. Dr Fredericks and the alarming Professor Cavalli had already decided everything before ever she was sent round to the professor's hotel.

It annoyed her. It worried her. She could not account for it, and that made her frightened. In other circumstances, she would have turned the job down. But now she not only needed the money, she had an imperative need to get out of Oxford fast.

Robert, having glimpsed her at the party, was clearly making considerable efforts to get in touch with her. He could not, of course, explain his interest in a girl who was neither a musician nor an undergraduate, so he was having to go very carefully. Because he was going so carefully, Sara had a little time to make her escape. But not a lot of time.

Mike, obviously amused, congratulated her on having made a conquest of the visiting composer. Sara had thanked him without expression.

'No really,' Mike said, interpreting her lack of reaction as disbelief, 'he keeps bringing your name up. Wants to know how well I know you. Wonders whether you play an instrument and would like to join the orchestra.'

Sara, as Robert well knew, played the oboe. She said nothing.

'Well, do you?' pursued Mike, his eyes sharp as a squirrel's.

'Do I want to play in the orchestra? No, I don't think so, Mike. I couldn't guarantee to be free for rehearsals, even if I ever got through the audition,' Sara told him politely.

'Mmm. Interesting,' he had observed, and left the kitchen table, whistling.

Sara was tempted to ask him not to tell Robert where she could be found and restrained herself. After all, he already knew where she was living. It could not matter very much if he discovered where she worked as well. Sooner or later, he would be able to track her down if he wanted to. And from Mike's hints it seemed that he wanted to.

Every time she walked round a corner in Oxford, she braced herself in case she bumped into Robert. She began to avoid the area where the orchestra had its rehearsal rooms, taking great detours if necessary to get from her office to the laboratories where she was sometimes called upon to work. Twice she glimpsed him in the distance. On each occasion, she fled blindly, stopping only when it occurred to her that the sight of her pelting through the street as if the devil were after her could only draw to herself the attention she was most anxious to avoid. Sara began to feel hunted.

Robert himself was clearly not trying to avoid her at all. She found herself invited to concerts and musical evenings to which nobody had ever asked her before. No matter whom the invitation came from, Sara was pretty certain that Robert was behind it. She was bewildered and very fearful of being hurt again.

Against her will, she found herself recalling the past. When she had first met Robert, she had been full of admiration, tongue-tied with shyness. When he asked her out she had been excited but more than a little frightened as well. It had only been gradually that she had relaxed with him. He had seemed immensely sophisticated, infinitely superior to the unfledged adolescent she still felt herself to be in those days.

He had taken her to fashionable cocktail parties, introducing her in a lordly fashion as if their hosts ought to be honoured that they had managed to persuade Robert and Sara to attend the party. Sara had been at first startled, then amused by this air of his. But there was no doubt that it added to her confidence.

If Robert loved and valued her, she felt she did not need to shrink from meeting anyone else, however important. For the first time in her life, she began to feel secure in the affection of another person. When they walked through the parks after rehearsals, and she put out a hand, Robert's was instantly there to take her own. She had been so happy. And Robert, in spite of his sophistication, had seemed happy too.

The only cause of dissension had been Sara's reluctance to sleep with him. At the time, he had been annoyed, and she herself had been puzzled. She loved him, she wanted him to be happy and have what he wanted. And he had manifestly wanted her. And yet, she had pulled back, turned away, rejected him. Half apologetically, it was true, but nevertheless unmistakably rejected him. Later she was glad of it. Later still, she wondered if that was partly why he had broken the engagement. If she had already been wholly committed to him, she reasoned, perhaps he would not have done so.

Yes, there was no doubt that the sooner she got out of Oxford and the disturbing sphere of Robert's influence, the sooner her peace of mind would return.

In her anxiety to quit Oxford, she did not allow herself to dwell on the undoubtedly peculiar circumstances in which her new job had come about. Dr Fredericks, normally too exalted and too vague to recognise his staff, much less remember their names, now regularly waved a friendly hand at her when they passed. And if they met on the stairs, he asked kindly after her health. Sara wondered uneasily what she had done to become so untypically memorable. Surely the professor would not have told Dr Fredericks what happened when they had met at that awful party? The very thought made her wince. But respectable academics would not discuss such things, she told herself with some desperation. Nevertheless, Dr Fredericks continued friendly and was helpfulness itself when Professor Cavalli finally decided that he was leaving for Venice in two days' time, and she had to accompany him. Mrs Templeton demurred, but Dr Fredericks overrode her objections and Sara found herself free at once.

Preparations were hectic. She had few enough personal possessions but those she had needed to be packed up and stored. And she had to tell Sir Gerald, her last remaining link with the old life, where she was going. And, through it all, the professor telephoned at odd moments, asking her to collect papers, buy books, deliver and receive messages. Afterwards she remembered those last thirty-six hours in Oxford as a blur in which she was perpetually breathless, permanently late and always sprinting between tasks.

She was even late at the airport.

Professor Cavalli was waiting for her at the check-in desk, and he did not look as if he was in a good mood. Sara doubted whether he had ever in his life been anxious about anything so he would clearly not worry about whether or not she turned up. But he clearly did not relish being kept waiting.

'Did you come by way of Beachy Head?' he asked with a mocking lift of one eyebrow.

Sara was flustered. 'No. I'm sorry. There was so much to do. . . .'

'There was?' The blue eyes glinted. 'Your packing can't have taken long, I imagine.' He picked up her small suitcase and balanced it mockingly on one finger. 'You travel light, don't you?'

For a moment, Sara had been angry. She was sensitive about her pathetically small wardrobe, her lack of personal possessions. She had never had anyone to give her things and she always felt that this solitariness was advertised to the world by the lack of clothes and small personal possessions that even the poorest of her fellow ballet students had owned. Now her eyes flashed before she recalled that the professor would have no way of knowing her lonely state.

She said in a colourless voice, 'I don't need much.'

He gave her a sharp look.

'You don't give much away, either, do you? What did I say to make you mad?'

She was startled and showed it. She was not used to encountering such perception.

'You looked as mad as a horse-fly,' he informed her kindly. 'Before you decided to keep it out of sight.'

She had said nothing and refused to meet his eyes, looking instead across the tarmac beyond the huge windows to where a number of aeroplanes stood.

'All right,' he had said, his voice faintly edged with amusement. 'We'll let the matter drop. For the moment.'

Recalling that little exchange as the plane touched down, Sara shivered. In spite of his good humour, she detected an iron determination in the professor, as if he were used to getting his own way in everything, no matter how trivial, and was not going to be balked by an insignificant, imported secretary. It made her feel faintly threatened but it also roused her temper. Normally, she was a sweet-natured girl, but this man was beginning to tap stores of resentment that she had not previously known she possessed.

She followed him out of the plane, outwardly meek. But inwardly, she was more than half prepared for battle. If he made one more of his damned personal remarks, she promised herself vigorously, he would get more than he bargained for.

It was a small airport by Sara's standards. She had travelled to New York, San Francisco and Paris with the ballet company, but she had never been to Italy before. She looked round with interest and saw that the professor had found a friend.

He was deep in conversation with a superbly dressed woman that Sara could only describe to herself as a beauty. She had never heard him speak his native language before and the rapid Italian startled and slightly disconcerted her. It made him seem very much a stranger and herself isolated in a foreign land. She hovered at a distance, not wanting to interrupt.

The woman was doing most of the talking. Now she put a hand out and laid the palm flat against the front of his jacket. Sara, trained in the precise significance of the minutest movement, had no doubt at all as to what the gesture meant. The woman was telegraphing to anyone who might be interested that the professor was her property. Sara found that she was slightly surprised. He did not look like anyone's property.

An imperious arm waved her over to join him.

'Daniella, speak English,' he admonished his companion. 'This is Sara, since you're so interested in the subject.'

The woman introduced as Daniella gave a sniff.

'Sara, may I introduce our friend and neighbour, Signora Vecellio,' he added formally.

Sara murmured a greeting and was surprised by the hostile survey she received in return.

'I do not at all understand why Luigi needs a secretary,' the beauty announced. 'Particularly now when all his work is done. Anything that was necessary, I would have been happy to undertake. . . .'

She was interrupted by a great shout of laughter from the professor.

'Darling Daniella, I really cannot see you slaving over a hot typewriter. It would be so bad for your nails, for one thing.'

And he took the beautifully manicured hand from the front of his jacket and kissed the tips of her fingers before restoring it to her with a mischievous look. Sara thought that the signora would take umbrage at such blatant mockery but she did not. Instead, she pouted a little, and shook her fall of artlessly untidy hair in reproach.

'Oh Ben, you are impossible. But it will be so inconvenient for you!'

He looked sardonic. 'On the contrary, Daniella,' he said gently. 'I asked Sara to come to the Palazzo precisely because I thought it would be very convenient. For lots of reasons.'

Sara gave him a quick, surprised glance, but he was concentrating all his attention on the other woman. For some reason, the signora looked uncomfortable for a moment, but the expression was soon banished, and she was chattering in excited Italian again.

'English,' he commanded.

She made a face, but obeyed, saying in charmingly accented English to Sara,

'I ask, how long you will be here.'

Sara was nonplussed. She had a strong feeling that her companion did not want her to tell the signora anything very specific, so she said calmly, 'For as long as it takes to finish the project, I imagine.'

The signora frowned.

'How is this? You do not know how long that will be?'

The professor interrupted before she could answer. 'Nobody could do more than guess at the moment, Daniella. Don't be silly. It will depend in part on Uncle Luigi and how long he wants the book to be. We are very lucky that Sara does not object to such a vague attitude to time.'

He smiled down at Sara. She was puzzled, and it must have shown in her face because his smile grew.

'Italians are not particularly conscious of the discipline of time,' he told her. 'As you will discover. And Uncle Luigi is more oblivious to it than most.'

'Well, they seem prompt enough in the airports, anyway,' she observed drily, pointing to the door at which a pile of luggage from their flight had appeared. 'Do you want me to collect it?' she added conscientiously, thinking he might prefer a few more words in private with the lovely Daniella.

'No,' he said, 'I'll get them and see you by the Customs line.'

Left facing Daniella, Sara shifted uncomfortably. There was no mistaking the other woman's suspicion. Though what she could be suspicious of, Sara could not begin to make out.

'The Palazzo Cavalli is remote,' she remarked, now, watching Sara closely. 'It will not be easy for your friends to visit. You would be more comfortable in a *pensione* in the city.'

'Oh, I have no friends in Italy,' Sara assured her.

The dark eyes snapped. 'Then why are you here? It cannot be much fun to work for a silly old man on an isolated sandbank. . . . Not for a young girl.'

Sara shrugged, and began walking towards the Customs official. The professor, she observed, had not only appropriated one of the few luggage trolleys, he had even found a porter to push it.

'It is ridiculous,' said Daniella, her high heels tapping angrily as she hurried along beside Sara. 'What is there here for you?'

Sara stopped, turned, and surveyed Signora Vesellio calmly.

'There is an excellent salary.'

Daniella gave another of her head tossings which made her look like a temperamental pony.

'You tell me you are here for the *money*?' she echoed.

They were at the professor's side. He was talking to a Customs Officer, but he looked round at that, and slanted an enigmatic glance at Daniella.

'Oh, you've found out Sara's secret so quickly, have you?'

'Secret?' Daniella turned to him, wide-eyed and kittenish.

'That she will do anything for money,' the professor said softly, raising a quizzical eyebrow at Sara, 'or, at least, that was what the product description claimed.'

Daniella looked suitably shocked. Sara lifted her chin and glared at him.

'I hope I haven't promised more than I can perform,' she told him sweetly. 'It is going to be difficult staying polite to you, even for money.'

There was an instant in which his brows drew together, and Sara caught a flash of expression which startled her. It was as if he were really, uncontrollably angry. Then his face changed, and he was laughing. She might have imagined the frown.

'I think it will be better if I do not insist on politeness, then,' he teased.

But it was not imagination, and Daniella knew it too. The Italian girl had obviously recognised that brief flare of temper. Looking from one to another, she made a discovery.

'I think you are not very—oh, what is it, the English say—fond, yes, that is it. I think you two are not very fond of each other.'

'I congratulate you on your perception, dearest Daniella,' drawled Professor Cavalli. 'I could never be—as the English do, indeed, say—*fond* of Sara Thorn. And I have little doubt that it is mutual.'

That was the moment at which the Customs Officer decided to wave through all the professor's luggage, and Sara's modest suitcase, so no more was said on the subject.

Sara followed him in rather subdued order. She could not help feeling that, in the battle of words between them, he had come off best. She had been insulting, of course, and she had done it deliberately, hoping to needle him out of his amusement. But he had really hurt.

It was extraordinary how much it hurt to know that he could never be fond of her. It was not surprising. It was not even unexpected. And God knows she did not want to get involved with any man again. So it was quite unreasonable that she should flinch from that casual announcement of his, or that reaction to it should leave her cold and a little tremulous as if she had burned herself.

A uniformed man was waiting for them on the other side of Passport Control and Customs. At first, Sara did not believe that he could be anything other than a king's chauffeur, so immaculate was his uniform, so exquisitely deferential his manner. But Professor Cavalli greeted him breezily as Salvatore, and instructed him to put all the luggage, including that belonging to Signora Vecellio, in the boat. Sara's Italian was limited, but it was enough to identify the vehicle. She showed her surprise.

Daniella was faintly pitying. 'Everyone uses boats in Venice. You can't take a car further than the Piazzale Roma. It is all canals and little rivers, anyway, so there would be no point. And Ben, of course, lives out in the lagoon like a savage, and would be quite marooned without a boat.'

Sara made no reply because Daniella was instructing the professor to pay the *facchino* in charge of her own mountain of matched luggage. During the ensuing voyage, Daniella ignored her.

It left Sara time to contemplate. She thought of Sir Gerald as she had last seen him, concern etched in every line of his dramatic face. He was the nearst thing she had to a family, and certainly he was the only person now who cared whether she ever danced again.

Sir Gerald was a dancer of the old school, born into a long line of dancers. He had inherited a small company from his father who had—as he was fond of telling his friends—danced for the Tzar of all the Russias—and built it up into one of the most respected international dance companies in the world.

When she was healthy, Sara had seen little of him. He was remote from the concerns of the *corps de ballet*, too magnificent to bestow more than an occasional word of encouragement upon a young dancer. He would sweep into final rehearsals, tall in a cartwheel hat and ankle-length cloak, drill them all rigorously until they thought they would faint from weariness, and then, right at the last moment, tell them, with his famous smile, that they were wonderful, truly wonderful.

Until she was ill, she had been a little afraid of him. Then, however, she had learned of his true kindness of heart. He had visited her frequently, bringing her little bunches of violets and lilies of the valley, just as he had done in the days when she danced for him. When she came out of hospital, he had regularly summoned her to his dark and untidy flat for tea poured out of a massive pot of chased silver which the grateful Tzar had presented to his father.

It was only to Sir Gerald that she had mentioned her misgivings about the job in Venice. He had more than shared them. His dramatic imagination suggested to him all sorts of dire possibilities. These he had retailed to Sara.

'You make it sound as if I'm bound for the white slave trade,' she protested.

'How do you know you're not?' countered Sir Gerald darkly.

'But—well— Ben Cavalli isn't that sort of man.' She had a sudden devastating vision of the firm mouth and brilliant, laughing eyes. 'He wouldn't lie. If he was going to make you do something you didn't want to do, he'd tell you, and dare you to oppose him. But he wouldn't deceive you,' she said positively.

Sir Gerald, beginning to entertain another scenario, looked obscurely pleased and said no more, beyond advising her not to forget to keep Dermott Andrews posted of her whereabouts.

Sir Gerald, who knew Andrews to be the foremost specialist in his field, had absolute confidence in him, while Sara, her hopes dashed so many times, now simply refused to think about it at all. The latest suggestion, to Sir Gerald's great glee and her own trepidation, was a course of treatment in Switzerland. According to Mr Andrews it had worked in the case of a young footballer. There was no reason why it should not work for herself. He was sending her notes to the clinic, having already discussed her case with the visiting specialist when he was lecturing at Oxford.

It was after her interview with Mr Andrews that Sara had encountered Chris who had taken pity on her look of white misery. The trouble was that she was almost certain that, even if this treatment was more hopeful than any of the others which Mr Andrews had suggested, there was still the almost insuperable problem of expense. She had been saving hard but, even so, she could not begin to afford the cost of treatment that Mr Andrews had mooted in America. There was every reason to believe that this Swiss scheme would prove the same.

Under the seat Sara flexed her left foot, rotating it as Mr Andrews had instructed. It was stiff after the flight and hurt a little. It seemed unlikely that it would ever be strong enough to dance on.

She turned her head to look out into the spray-strewn seascape. She would not think about it. There was nothing she could do. At least, she amended, there was nothing she could do for the moment. And Venice approached.

She looked about her with delight as the little boat sped down canals that previously she had only read about. It was like something out of a fairytale, an improbable back cloth of terracotta palaces alternating with ornate stone and even marble. The window embrasures were long and dark and it was easy to imagine the mediaeval nobles who had once lurked behind them, watching the traffic on the canals.

The brilliant sun struck diamond sparks from water and stone alike. Sara saw a cat dozing in careless splendour on a curlicued balcony of a particularly magnificent palazzo. It yawned as they passed. Everywhere the sun was evident: turning stone to apricot and honey, the canal water to shimmering, shifting wonder, so that it looked like liquid light. And, where the shadow of a bridge or a building crossed their path, it was as black and sharp as if it were a hole suddenly punched in that glorious fabric of light. Sara felt her throat tighten at the beauty of it.

And, marvelling at the sumptuous beauty of this unexpected city, Sara took a decision. Far too long she had been bewildered, unhappy, torn between hope and the fear of hope. None of it had done her any good and her life, as a result, had dwindled to her recent grey existence. It was impossible to imagine anything in Venice being grey. Even wretched Sara Thorn, she thought ruefully, would be compelled to take the tint of gold with which the city was touched.

She would not resist it. More, she would revel in it. Venice reached out to her and she responded. She had, she knew, refused to allow herself to be moved by the beauties of Oxford. She would not make the same mistake here.

And as for the past—well, it was the past, and could not be changed. Maybe it could not be forgotten either. If she could, she would go back and not let Robert into her life, reject Ben Cavalli's approach. At the memory of that passionate embrace, Sara felt her muscles tense and she bit her lip. Well, she could not alter that either, no matter how much she might be ashamed of herself and wish it undone. But she could, if she chose, put it out of her mind, at least for the moment.

For the moment, she was going to give herself wholly

to Venice. The past could stay in the past and the future was something which she would not allow herself to contemplate. The moment was everything and she was going to savour it.

The motor suddenly cut and Sara jumped. She had not noticed that they had drawn up to the side of the canal and were now bobbing gently at a landing stage as Daniella disembarked gracefully. She kissed Ben Cavalli on the mouth.

'Ciao, caro,' she said and then, her eyes resting briefly on Sara, reverted to English for the last time. 'When Mario returns you must bring Sara to dinner. Mario will love to show off his English to someone who will be really impressed.'

The words were oddly spiteful. Sara was puzzled, wondering whether an insult was intended to herself or the unknown English speaker.

'Mario?' she asked, as Salvatore pulled on the starter and the engine roared back into life. 'Who is Mario, Professor Cavalli?' Sara repeated more loudly now that she was in competition with the engine.

He fell into the seat beside her and brought all his attention back from Daniella's suitcases abandoned on the canal side to Sara's face. She jumped at the sudden switch in intensity and he began to smile.

'Professor?' he murmured. 'Is that not a little formal? We are not in Oxford now. I would be much more comfortable if you called me by my given name.'

Sara withdrew along the leather-covered seat.

'I don't think that would be a very good idea,' she said, sounding, even to her own ears, impossibly prim.

The blue eyes mocked her.

'Don't you?' He put out a hand and just touched her cheek with one long finger. She jumped and he smiled. 'Why?'

The blue eyes were mesmerising, Sara thought in confusion. She felt her colour rise and was furious with herself. It was no wonder he found her amusing if she blushed like a schoolgirl every time he looked at her.

'Well—because—after all, you're my employer.' she said floundering.

He chuckled. 'Yes, I am aren't I? And that means that you have to do what I tell you. And I'm telling you to call me Ben.'

Sara was backing off as hard as she could. The edge of the arm rest was digging into the small of her back. She took a deep breath and tried to collect her thoughts.

'I would find it very difficult,' she explained, avoiding his eyes.

He was stroking her cheek with the back of his finger, as if he were feeling the quality of material, she thought indignantly. Her indignation did not prevent her from trembling with other emotions in response to that wickedly tantalising touch.

'Difficult?' he murmured softly. 'Why?'

'The—the sudden change,' she said wildly. 'The discontinuity. When one has started a relationship on a formal basis. . . .'

'Formal?' He made a great pantomime of surprise and disapproval. 'My dear girl, you will have to watch your step in Italy. We are very conservative, you know, and I don't think your idea of formality will be quite what my countrymen are used to.'

Sara flushed deeply. 'You know what I mean,' she muttered.

'Do I?' His eyes glinted. 'And yet I recall an incident or two in Oxford in which I would not think of describing either my behaviour or your own as formal.'

Staring at him in indignation, Sara suddenly discovered she could turn his own words against him.

'But we are not in Oxford now,' she countered.

'No, thank God. A fact of which I have the intention of taking every advantage. So be warned.'

Sara eyed him warily. 'Are you threatening me?'

He considered that, his head on one side.

'Not quite,' he decided after a pause. 'Call it a friendly piece of advice. . . . Look at it this way—if you insist on calling me professor under my own roof, I could beat you black and blue. I don't say I will; just that I could.'

Sara smiled. Wary though she was of him and his bright-eyed mockery, she did not fear physical violence on his part.

'I call that a fair warning,' she told him solemnly.

'Good. Bear it in mind. It's the last you'll get.'

He leaned back, folding his hands at the back of his neck and stretching like a cat in the sun. The little boat had left the narrow canals again and was once more in the open lagoon. The water was choppy and the boat bounced. It was to be hoped, Sara thought wryly, that she was not sick before she arrived at their destination. She did not know how her unpredictable new employer would react to a nauseous secretary. She concentrated hard on a configuration of birds in the sky and tried to ignore her churning stomach.

The professor had not appeared to notice her discomfort. Now, his eyes still apparently closed, he spoke.

'You're very pale. Did the flight disagree with you?'

She slewed round, startled, and stared at him. One blue eye opened lazily and mocked her.

'I—I feel a bit funny,' she acknowledged unwillingly. 'I didn't realise you'd noticed.'

He closed his eyes again and stretched his arms pleasurably above his head.

'Aeroplanes are nasty, cramped things. It's not surprising if you feel unwell. And as for noticing—you must have realised by now that I notice every move you make.'

Sara gasped. It sounded as if he meant that last

remark, even though it was said lightly. She shivered. If he were going to watch her all the time, she would never feel at ease. She stole a look at him. He seemed perfectly relaxed, not hostile. She decided to dare a question.

'Why?' she swallowed and, when he didn't answer at once, added rather sadly, 'Don't you trust me?'

He replaced his darkened glasses which he had removed when saying goodbye to Daniella.

'Does he trust you?' he countered in a neutral tone.

Sara was bewildered. 'He?'

'The irate fiancé,' he elaborated softly. 'The man you left behind.'

'Oh!' she flinched. Her companion, as quick as a cat, took note of the tiny movement.

'Are you running away from him?'

Sara looked away, out across the foam-flecked greyness to where the birds soared.

'In a way,' she said unwillingly.

He considered that. 'Only in a way?' he echoed thoughtfully. 'Does he know you're here?' He paused, and then added deliberately, 'With me?'

Sara flushed. 'I'm not *with* you,' she protested. 'Not—not in the way you make it sound.'

'The way anyone could make it sound,' he pointed out. 'Certainly, anyone who was at that party and saw us.' He paused. 'And anyway, aren't you?'

She looked at him indignantly. 'You know I'm not.'

'Well. Perhaps.' He was still staring at the sky. His mouth twisted a little. 'Though, as I warned you before, you would be very unwise to blind yourself to the possibilities. Still, I infer that you have not told him where you've gone.'

Sara shuddered at the thought, not needing to reply. Some day she would have to meet Robert again, to talk commonplaces, to pretend that they were no more and never had been more than remote acquaintances. . . . But she could not do it yet; not while the wound was still raw. Later, when she had found herself a new career, or even, by some miracle, had the old one restored to her, then she would meet him. When the pain of Robert's betrayal was no longer fresh in her mind, she would be able to meet him with composure. But now, while it was still so close, she could not. The devastation of her career was too intimately tied up with Robert's desertion. She could face one, but not both.

Her face must have revealed her thoughts because the professor sat up sharply.

'Why do you look like that? Are you afraid of him?'

Tears stung her eyes. His tone was incredulous, as if he could not believe that anybody could be so cowardly as to be afraid of someone else. She shook her head.

'You don't understand.'

'So explain,' he said softly.

'I—I rather gave you the wrong idea,' she said stiltedly. 'When I—when you——'

'When I started to make love to you,' he supplied coolly.

She bit her lip, looking away from him. 'I—yes.'

'So? What wrong idea did you give me?'

'When Robert knocked on the door,' she muttered. 'When I said we were engaged. It wasn't true.'

'What?'

'It was an explosive sound. Sara shrank. She had the impression, though the dark glasses did a good deal to hide his expression, that it was the last thing he had expected her to say. And that it had infuriated him.

'W-we had been engaged,' she hurried on, stammering. 'Before. W-we broke it off. I hadn't seen him for months. Not until that party. And I did not expect to see him there. It was a shock. That's partly why. . . .' She broke off.

'Why you let me come to your room?'

'I had to get away,' she said miserably.

'Why you would have let me make love to you?'

Sara could not look at him. 'I'd had a lot to drink,' she said in not much more than a whisper. She felt bitterly ashamed. 'More than I'm used to. It went to my head.'

'Are you trying to say you didn't know what you were doing?' he asked.

She drew a deep breath. 'No. No, but I was—oh, how can I say it? How can I put it so that you will understand?—I was unlike myself. I've never behaved like that before in my life.' She forced herself to turn towards him, meeting those masked eyes with resolution. 'I don't know why it happened.'

There was a long silence. The boat lolloped on. Salvatore's back to them, as rigid and unresponsive as if they had not been there. Sara wondered whether he spoke English and, if he did, whether he could hear their low conversation above the throb of the engine She cast him a worried look.

At once, her companion reached out and turned her face by the chin back towards himself.

'You don't know why it happened?' he echoed very softly. It was a tone that froze Sara to the marrow.

She looked at him steadily. 'No, I don't.'

For a fraction of a second, his fingers tightened cruelly. Then he released her and turned away, almost as if he were casting her off.

'Then you will have to learn. I shall take it upon myself to see that you do,' he said.

The mockery was blatant and edged with a hint of cruelty. Sara looked down at her lap where her hands were twining restlessly. It was a sure sign, she thought remotely. No matter how she tried, her hands always gave her away. Now, anyone that knew her would know that, in spite of her calm manner, she was on the edge of panic. It was an odd thought that this man, having encountered her so briefly, should nevertheless be someone whom she was sure could interpret those telltale movements. Sara wondered if she would ever be able to hide her thoughts from him or if her body would always betray her to those observant eyes.

'Why was it broken off?' he asked abruptly.

'W-what?' she said, startled out of her black reverie.

'The engagement. The previously absent fiancé. Who broke it off?'

She winced. 'He did,' she said in a clipped voice.

'So.' He took off the dark glasses and submitted her to a complete inspection from top to toe with insulting deliberation. 'And why? Why did a man who is obviously still crazy about you break off the engagement? What had you done?'

But she could not bear that. She flung up a hand as if to ward him off, not caring that it must look like some sort of admission of guilt.

He gave a harsh sigh. 'Well, perhaps it doesn't matter. I can see how you would drive a man crazy.'

She raised her head. She was almost beyond speech, but she managed to whisper, 'Please . . . don't judge me by—that night. I was shocked—desperate. There were other things. . . .'

'What other things?'

But she had done. She shook her head helplessly, knowing that if she tried to answer him, her command over her voice would give way and she would be unable to prevent the tears falling. She looked at him mutely, pleading in silence for understanding, or, if not understanding, some measure of mercy. He stared back implacably for a long minute.

Then he said, as if he were taking a vow, 'I swear that one day you will tell me. Of your own free will. Everything there is to tell.'

CHAPTER FOUR

THE view from her window was desolate. Sara looked out across the grey waters and wondered if this could possibly be the jewelled city of legend. Now that the canals and bridges, squares and palaces had been left behind, she felt very isolated. Between the gun-metal sky and the wheeling gulls, she shivered.

Sara turned away from the window. She felt off balance, alarmed, half excited. She did not understand the professor; and here, while the gulls keened and the water slapped steadily against the sides of boat and jetty under her window, his threat to woo her secrets out of her suddenly seemed more dangerous. It had probably been no more than a joke—and yet—and yet. . . .

There was a rudimentary knock on her door, and then the manservant who had met them at the jetty appeared with her single suitcase. He bestowed a fatherly smile upon her, giving her no hint, by his manner, that Sara's luggage was less than he was accustomed to bringing upstairs for lady guests. He placed it carefully on a stool at the far end of the immensely high, damask-hung room, and beamed at her.

'Thank you,' she said shyly, 'but I could have brought it up myself.'

'It is nothing, signorina. The path from the boathouse can be treacherous.'

She nodded ruefully. 'You have a point there. But you mustn't feel you have to wait on me.'

The smile widened. 'But it will be a pleasure, signorina. The *signore* wants you to feel at home here.'

Sara's eyes flew involuntarily to that oddly fascinating landscape.

'I think I shall,' she said slowly, wonderingly. Then she gave herself a little shake; she had sounded almost frightened for the moment. 'Especially, when you speak such good English. Is everyone here as fluent? I'm sorry, I don't know your name.'

'I am, Guilio, signorina,' he informed her benevolently. 'And yes, we all speak English—even Vittoria. Except when she is in a temper and then she throws plates. She is the cook. But it was necessary to speak English to the signore's mother. The Principessa is American, and at first, she didn't speak any Italian at all.'

Sara was puzzled. She had been warned about isolation. She had been given to understand that there was only the professor and his Uncle Luigi on the islet, apart from the servants. Was there, after all, another woman to whom she could talk?

'Principessa?' she queried.

Guilio looked a little uncomfortable, like a good servant who has been caught out in gossip.

'The mother of Signor Benedetto,' he explained.

'His mother is here?' asked Sara hopefully.

'Alas, no. No longer. Though she comes to visit, of course. She travels a good deal, I believe.'

'Will she visit soon, while I'm here?'

Guilio looked even more uneasy. 'Who can say? The Principessa is very restless, very social. She travels with her husband sometimes, and he does not like to come here. . . .'

Sara's eyebrows rose. 'The professor's father is still alive, then?'

Guilio visibly relaxed. Whatever question he had been expecting next it was not that one. It was clear that he had no trouble at all in talking about the professor's father.

'Ah no, signorina. Signor Mario died many years ago, when Signor Benedetto was just a boy. He was away at school then, and Signor Luigi came back all the way from Tibet to break the news to him. It was a bad time for the family. The Palazzo was shut up and we all went to Rome with the Principessa. Then she began to travel and to marry. . . .'

He broke off, looking annoyed with himself. Sara was intrigued. It was an odd way to put things. She found herself wondering how many times the Principessa had married in the intervening years. It would obviously be the height of inconsideration to ask Guilio. He was already fussing with the heavy curtains on the fourposter bed.

'So, we did not return here until Signor Benedetto opened the Palazzo again two years ago.'

'Only two years ago?' Sara echoed.

'*Si*. It was after the accident of Signor Luigi,' confided Guilio, cheerful again. He looped back the right-hand curtain with a gold-tasselled cord and gave it a little professional shake.

'Signor Benedetto said that it was impossible that he should continue to live quite alone and that he must be sensible. But Signor Luigi did not like to be told to be sensible. Oh, there was a battle. But, in the end, they agree—Signor Luigi is to live in the Palazzo all the time because it is very nearly isolated; and Signor Benedetto is to live here too when he is not in Switzerland.'

Sara watched in awe as Guilio, having looped the other curtain to his satisfaction, deftly whipped back the damask coverlet and folded it across the end of the bed.

'Switzerland?' she prompted. If her tormentor were to depart to Swizerland and leave her with just the author and his manuscript, life would be a good deal more peaceful.

'*Si. Il signore* has,' Guilio hesitated, 'business interests in Switzerland. Of course, he travels a lot, too, giving his lectures.'

'So he won't be here all that much,' mused Sara, more to herself than to the manservant.

Guilio beamed at her. 'Oh no, you must not think you will be alone, signorina. Normally, it is true, Signor Benedetto comes and goes as he wishes but he will not do so with a guest in the house.'

He gave her a little bow, twitching the coverlet to ensure that it lay draped perfectly, and went to the doors, swinging them both open with a flourish. Sara could have stamped her foot in frustration.

'I am not,' she said with considerable emphasis, 'a guest. I am here to work.'

'*Si*, signorina,' said Guilio placidly. 'You work very hard, for Signor Luigi.' She received another of his benevolently paternal looks. 'And for Signor Benedetto, you are a very charming guest.'

And he closed the doors firmly on whatever protest she might have found further voice to make.

In spite of the manservant's obvious friendliness, Sara found the whole conversation far from reassuring. There was that implicit assumption that she was here for the professor's amusement. The fact that Guilio, at least, seemed warmly in favour of the arrangement was no consolation to her.

She moved restlessly around her apartment, picking up objects, and putting them down again, without really having looked at them. She was, she realised, distinctly apprehensive. She had never before received the sort of attention that Ben Cavalli seemed determined to exert. He had no scrap of respect for her—he thought she was a slut and only interested in money—but he had told her that she was a puzzle that intrigued him. And he could take her into passion at his touch. It would be very easy for him to damage her beyond repair.

Sara went out on to the balcony. He was a potent threat to her peace of mind but not, she told herself, irresistible. She had months of independent restraint to arm her. And in the meantime, she would immerse herself in her job and its beautiful surroundings.

In the slanting rays of the dying sun, filtered through smoke-grey clouds, the lagoon looked peaceful, unearthly. There was a sharp tang of salt in the air and a faint breeze lifted her red hair and stirred it. Sara closed her eyes in delight.

She went down to the salotto on the stroke of nine. She had dressed very carefully in a dark green dress that made her skin look impossibly white. The auburn hair was swept up in a coronet above the upstanding, starched white collar of the dress.

She looked, she hoped, unobtrusive. Although nobody could look truly unobtrusive when they had to descend an enormous curving marble staircase that spanned two floors. Waiting for her in the hall were Guilio and a tall man in an ancient dinner jacket. Sara paused, uncertain, at the last flight.

It was, she thought like something out of one of the Christmas pantomime ballets. She should be coming down this staircase on *pointe*, dressed in glittering white, carrying a wand, or, perhaps, a fan. And a dashing young prince would surge forward to meet her and they would waltz off round the stage.

Her hand trembled and, for a moment, to the consternation of the men in the hall, it seemed as if she would cry. Then, she took herself in hand. Any ballerina, Sara told herself sternly, expecting to dance across seventeenth-century marble, would certainly be rewarded with a broken ankle. And she would probably succeed in bringing her prince tumbling down with her, Sara added sternly to herself. It was all a highly foolish fantasy. At the pictures she had conjured up, her green eyes began to twinkle.

'Signorina Thorn?'

The man in the dinner jacket came forward slowly. His carriage was upright but he moved as if with difficulty and, at the bottom of the staircase, stood with his hand resting on the bannister as if he needed its support.

She smiled shyly. 'Signor Cavalli?'

He was really remarkably like his nephew. There was the same height, the same firm mouth and proud profile. Only the older man's eyes were different, grey and less intense than those she had become all too familiar with. She gave him her hand.

'Luigi Cavalli, at your service, signorina. I am glad to welcome you to the Palazzo Cavalli and hope you will be very happy with us,' he said warmly. 'I was resting when you arrived or I should have joined you for tea. I hope you were well looked after?'

Sara assured him that everything that could possibly be done for her comfort had been performed. He looked pleased.

'Good. Excellent. It may be lonely for you here, you know. I want you to be as comfortable as possible. Anything you want you have only to ask Guilio.'

She thanked him again, a little overwhelmed by all this attention to a mere secretary.

'Then we will eat now, if that suits you, signorina. When we are on our own, we eat in the breakfast room, close to the kitchen. The dining room is too far away from the kitchen for convenience. Though of course we use it for formal dinner parties or when all the family are here.'

He led the way stiffly to a white-appointed room full of modern prints on the walls where tall sash windows looked out over a stone terrace and the sea beyond. In spite of the dark, the shutters were not closed and Sara could hear the hushing noise of the sea slapping against the stone walls.

Luigi went to the head of the table, and gestured her to sit at his right. Guilio bustled round the table and lit a branch of candles in the centre, before taking his place at the serving hatch at the end of the room.

There followed a prolonged and ceremonious meal. Sara, tired and more than a little disconcerted by the formality, would have been utterly tongue-tied had it not been for the practised charm of her host. He kept up a gentle flow of anecdote and history about the Palazzo throughout the first course and, by the time an exquisite dish of tiny grilled trout was served, she found herself talking to him as easily as if she had known him all her life. Indeed, in many ways, he reminded her of Sir Gerald. Soon, almost without her noticing that the tenor of the conversation had changed, he was asking her questions about herself and she was telling him with all the trust of long friendship.

'Your family are happy to lose you for so long?' he asked, sipping at pale golden wine and looking at her with remarkable shrewdness over the top of his glass. 'They perhaps encourage you to travel?'

She looked away. 'I am an orphan.'

He nodded calmly, as if that was what he had been expecting. 'But you have uncles, aunts, cousins?'

Sara shook her head. 'Not that I know of.'

Signor Luigi looked shocked. 'But that is not possible! You are quite alone? Unprotected? How then do you live? How were you brought up?'

'In an orphanage,' Sara said frankly. 'It was a good one, and everybody was very kind. They took lots of trouble to make sure that the girls and boys followed their own bent. Though, sometimes, with such a lot of us, it was very inconvenient.' She thought of Mrs Maxwell driving her every morning into York to go to ballet classes before dashing back to oversee the little ones' reading classes. 'But they managed.'

He seemed touched. 'So you have no home?'

She shrugged. It was a question she had been asked before and answering it honestly no longer gave her the pain it once had.

'I've lived in a succession of rented rooms. I can usually make myself comfortable quite quickly with my books and my radio.'

He filled her glass.

'While you are here, you are to regard the Palazzo as entirely your home,' he instructed. 'And—as you are not already oversupplied with relatives and I have no niece—you will call me Uncle Luigi.'

That startled her.

'Oh, but—surely that would not be very respectful?'

Uncle Luigi sat back in his white wicker chair and extracted a cigarette case from his pocket. He made a great fuss about extracting a cigarette, tapping it rhythmically on the tablecloth and then fitting it into an ebony holder. After this delicate operation had been accomplished to his satisfaction, he spoke again.

'My dear child, when you have seen my untidy manuscripts and truly horrible writing, you will not *want* to be respectful.' The note of irony was so like his nephew's that Sara blinked.

She laughed, at once at ease again. 'Oh, I'm used to deciphering awful writing. I think it must be something to do with being an academic, this inability to write properly. In my experience, the more eminent they are, the worse they scrawl. I suppose it is because your head is so full of ideas that your handwriting can't keep up with your brain?' she ended on an interrogative note.

She encountered a dry look.

'I am hardly qualified to say, my dear Sara. I am neither eminent nor an academic. Just an old man with a hobby. Although my scheming nephew may have told you otherwise.'

'He said you had prepared a catalogue of the family's collection of maps which was also a thesis for a doctorate,' she explained.

Uncle Luigi snorted through his fine patrician nose.

'That is nonsense. And Ben knows it. I ran away

from school at fourteen and have never been inside an establishment of learning since. No university of any self-respect would give me a doctorate.' There was an unmistakable tinge of bitterness to the light voice. 'I was happy enough to catalogue the collection because it really needed to be done. Though I know that Ben arranged it as a sort of therapy for me. And taking all the maps out of the bank vault and bringing them to the Palazzo must have cost him a fortune. Not least, in insurance. But as for academic honours——' he shook his head. 'It is too late for that now. Fifty years too late.'

They were interrupted by Guilio bringing in a tureen of some sort of stew, redolent of garlic and herbs and lemon juice. He set it down on a heated tray and ladled a generous portion on to a gold-edged plate which he set in front of Sara. He served her host and then left.

'But enough of me,' said Luigi Cavalli, leaning forward with a charming smile to pour more wine into her glass. 'You are a witch, little Sara. You make me talk about myself when I want to learn about you. Are you the champion typist of theses? Is that what you always wanted to do with your life when you were in your orphanage?'

'I don't think it is what anyone would have wanted to do all their life,' she said composedly, 'but it's rewarding to do it well.'

'If you can't do what you really want to, eh?' he prompted shrewdly.

'How many of us do that?' she countered.

'Some. The reckless ones. I did.'

Sara found she was not surprised. He still had that slightly reckless air about him. She smiled.

'I did exactly what I wanted to,' he told her with pride. 'As a result I was the black sheep of the family. They didn't like having a wanderer discredit the family name, you see. They were all good businessmen. Had been for generations. A doge every fifty years, they used to say, was a Cavalli. And there was Luigi running off to China without so much as finishing his schooling.'

'China?' She was fascinated. 'When did you go to China? I thought it was forbidden to foreigners.'

'So it is, from time to time. When I went there, it was in the middle of a Civil War and nobody was in much of a position to enforce any ban on anyone.'

'Do you speak Chinese?' she asked.

'Which Chinese?' he teased, his eyes glinting in a way that made him look uncomfortably like his nephew. 'I can be pompous in Mandarin and make myself understood in Cantonese. Though it's always a mistake to make yourself too clearly understood in China.' He pushed his untouched plate away from him in disgust, as if it was the People's Republic of China in person. 'Mao would have got on very well with my mother,' he announced viciously. 'Damned busybody, with no respect for anyone.'

Sara thought it prudent not to enquire whether this description was to be applied to the statesman, her host's mother, or, as she very much suspected, both at the same time.

'She was a very domineering woman, my mother,' Uncle Luigi went on undeterred. 'Ruined my brother's life with her matchmaking. Would have ruined mine if I'd given her half a chance. And damn nearly finished Ben's.'

Sara found that she was suddenly compulsively interested in the doings of Uncle Luigi's mother. She swallowed hard and forebore to say so. Her host, however, seemed to be in the telling vein.

'Had a girl all picked out for him. Silly thing, thought she wanted to be an actress. Her father was a banker and she was his sole heir so my mother thought she was ideal. Public engagement, big party—then, six months later, she runs away with this movie actor. That was when he went to America. He never said, of course, but

I think he was badly hurt. She was a little slut, but he was fond of her, and she had made him look a damned fool. What he did say, when his grandmother started her matchmaking again was that his experience of nice girls was enough to put him off them for life.' Uncle Luigi gave a chuckle. 'She didn't like that,' he said with satisfaction. 'Screamed at him that if he went on like that he'd never marry because no nice girl would have him: and he came right back and said that he had no intention of marrying then or ever. I thought she'd burst,' he remembered pleasurably.

'I infer from the satisfaction with which you speak that you are boring Sara with tales of my grandmother,' said a cool voice behind them.

Sara flushed, embarrassed to be caught gossiping about him with his uncle. Ben Cavalli strolled forward, eyeing with interest the flushed cheeks and self-conscious expression.

Uncle Luigi chuckled. 'It hasn't been boring these last twenty years, thanks to you and me. And your mother, I suppose.'

'My mother is too afraid of being bored to allow herself to become boring,' Ben agreed lightly. He looked round the table. 'Have you not finished yet?'

Sara was almost certain that he had changed the subject deliberately. Uncle Luigi, however, seemed to notice nothing. 'No, I've been talking too much and Sara has very kindly been listening with patience.'

She smiled at him. 'I don't think you've been talking too much at all.'

He looked at his nephew. 'See what I mean? Patience personified.'

Ben smiled but, to Sara's eyes, it seemed a little forced. She wondered if he did not like to see his uncle being so friendly to her. Ben himself had shown no signs of wanting to be treated respectfully, but he might exact different standards on his uncle's behalf, she thought.

Uncle Luigi seemed not to notice. 'Now you're here, you can have some of Vittoria's almond and apple flan,' he informed his nephew. 'She made it especially for you and was most put out when Guilio said you wouldn't be at dinner.'

At that Ben smiled without a shadow. 'Plates thrown in the kitchen?' he enquired. 'Must I make my peace?'

'Certainly, by ringing Guilio and telling him we'll have the sweet now and you will join us for it,' his uncle said firmly.

Ben obeyed, smiling.

For the rest of the meal, Sara barely spoke. Uncle and nephew seemed on excellent terms and the conversation did not flag. Anxious not to intrude, she nibbled at the rich pastry she did not want, and listened to their exchange. They were both witty and had the same sense of humour, and she found their company highly entertaining. The only sour note was struck when Uncle Luigi, replenishing Ben's glass, said casually.

'Did you eat out?'

Ben gave him a swift, shrewd look before saying evenly, 'I had some work to catch up on.'

'After you got back to the Palazzo?' pursued his uncle.

'As you say.'

'Why did you go back to the town so soon after your arrival?' asked Uncle Luigi, idly cracking a walnut.

'I had to see someone.'

Uncle Luigi's lips tightened at that unrevealing answer.

'Daniella Vecellio?'

Ben's brows met above his nose in a ferocious frown. Sara thought she would have been terrified if he looked at her like that. Uncle Luigi appeared unmoved.

'I do not know how you can allow yourself . . .' he said in tones of disgust.

But Ben stopped him. 'It is bad enough to bore poor

Sara with family *history*; present domestic disagreements are quite unforgivable.'

His uncle stopped dead. The heavy brows, so like Ben's own, rose, and he surveyed Sara slowly as if he had only just realised that she was still sitting there. Slowly he began to smile. Ben looked, if anything, even more angry than he had done before.

'I was forgetting,' Uncle Luigi said. He took Sara's hand and squeezed it gently. 'You will forgive me, little one? You will not be upset by my private disagreements with my nephew?'

Ben, Sara saw in a quick look under her lashes, wore a thunderous expression.

'Oh, it's none of my business,' she said hurriedly. 'In fact, I was thinking I had better leave you to discuss it in private. I'm very tired and. . . .'

'Nonsense!' said the elder Cavalli, giving her hand another squeeze before letting it go. 'You are being tactful. But it is absolutely no use being tactful with me, my dear. I have no sensibilities left. And as for Ben, I don't think he ever had any.'

At this insult, his nephew palpably relented. The steely look left his eyes and he grinned.

'I take after my uncle,' he retorted. 'No sensitivity and less tact.'

His uncle threw up one hand in mock defence, leaning back in his chair as if to avoid a blow.

'You can't come browbeating me, my lad. I'm an old man,' he said. 'And,' with a wicked lift of the eyebrow, 'to demonstrate how *much* more tactful I am than yourself, I will now retire and leave you to make amends to Sara for this family brawling.' He turned smiling. 'Good night, my dear. Sleep well—when this ruffian lets you get to bed.'

He departed, leaving an odd silence in his wake. Sara could feel her heart beating lightly and too rapidly somewhere in the region of her throat. She swallowed and the sound seemed deafening in the silence. She dropped her eyes to her wine glass, still more than half full. Had she had too much wine? Was that what accounted for this trembling, this fear that she was on the brink of something strange and dangerous? She swallowed again.

Ben said abruptly, 'It's too hot in here. They must have forgotten to pull the blinds down this afternoon. We'll go out on the terrace.'

He led her through glass conservatory doors on to a paved area. She could see very little in the sudden darkness. It was very warm still, but the sky was overcast and she could only occasionally glimpse a star before the clouds covered it again.

'There's thunder in the air,' he remarked. 'We don't usually have skies like this in summer.' His voice sounded strained.

'It was so sunny earlier,' she remarked. If they kept on the subject of weather, perhaps the agitated beating of her pulses would subside to normal speed. 'And yet now. . . .'

'Didn't you see how it had greyed over when you were on the balcony?' Ben asked.

Sara went very still. She had thought herself alone. What had she done? She had gone to feed the gulls. It had been a moment of absolute privacy. In her solitude, unguarded, she had revealed—what? Had she perhaps danced a few steps? Let tears fall? She could not remember. But she knew she felt desperately intruded on, as if she had been naked to the unknown watcher.

She said in a voice she did not recognise. 'Where were you?'

Ben moved. He was beside her, very close, and she thought he was looking at her though she could not make him out clearly in the darkness. His arm brushed her shoulder. She thought she felt his breath on her hair but could not be sure.

'I was coming back from the city. I was in a boat. I just came round the point and saw you.'

Instead of slowing her pulses accelerated at his nearness. A deep secret tremor like an impending earthquake was making her whole body shudder imperceptibly. She felt that if he touched her she would shatter like glass. She moved away.

'I didn't know anyone was there,' she said. It came out high and breathless.

He gave a soft laugh. 'I know.'

'You spied on me,' she accused, whipping up anger to defeat the other nameless emotions that were threatening to engulf her. 'How could you? I may only be your employee, but I am still a human being. I have a right to my privacy.'

There was a chilling silence. Then he said, too civilly, 'Oh, quite.'

Something in his tone gave her a warning, and she flashed round to face him just as he reached out and took her in an implacable hold.

'And I, too,' he mocked, 'though I may only be your employer, am still a human being. And as such. . . .'

No, she thought frantically. *No.* But it was too unforeseen, too sudden, and there was that insidious trembling that she could not control. He had no difficulty at all in wrenching her off balance and into his arms.

It was more than a kiss, it was an invasion. Sara felt as if she had been thoroughly overcome, dispossessed of will and disposed of according to the victor's whim. For he was not gentle and he was not forbearing. It did not seem to occur to him that Sara was not the possessor of an experience equal to his own. Or if it occurred to him, he did not permit it to deflect him from his purpose. And it was very clear, even to a startled girl of limited experience, what that purpose was.

He pinioned her against him, so that she could feel

his blood racing as fast as her own. Holding her face between his hands he explored her mouth ruthlessly. The tantalising gentleness he had shown on the night of the party was gone and in its place was a raw demand that both thrilled and terrified her. He was forcing her—forcing her to accept the invasion of his tongue; forcing her to accept the shocking intimacy of his capture of her lower lip between his teeth; forcing her to respond. His mouth left hers and made its devastating way along her jaw and frail throat to her shoulder. Sara felt the material of her dress fall away as, with an intensity close to tenderness, he kissed the skin. A deep, sweet shudder shook her. She had never felt so helpless, so utterly pliant, so desired. Without shame, her own hands reached for him.

She had not known she could be capable of such wantonness. At its deepest core her body ached for him. She had never felt like this before, did not even know what it was that she was yearning towards, but she knew that she had wanted everything he was doing to her—and more. Ben raised his head and this time she met his mouth eagerly.

For a heart-stopping second there was nothing else in the whole whirling world, but their ardent blood and his heart, thudding like a steam hammer, driving her beyond the limit of her experience. Then he broke the kiss and stood for a moment, holding her hard against him.

'Sara,' he said softly, unsteadily. His mouth moved against her eyebrow. 'Lovely Sara, I want you so much.' He drew a shaky breath. 'God, how I want you!' He strained her against him. 'I never meant—I know it's too soon——'

Sara barely heard him. Realisation of where she was heading had burst upon her like one of the thunderclaps now making itself heard in the distance. She might be innocent, but she was not a fool, and she knew that the smouldering pleasure she felt in his arms would need only the slightest breath to fan it into a flame which would consume her utterly.

She raised her hand to his chest and pushed herself gently away from him. His hands immediately came up to clasp her own warmly against him.

She swallowed, trying to retreat, trying for a normal tone. Across the lagoon, a shaft of lightning forked with shocking suddenness.

'It's going to rain,' she said in her best conversational manner. The weather was going to have to bail her out of this difficulty.

Ben did not seem to notice her resistance. He gave a low, rueful laugh.

'Yes, we can't stay out here much longer. And I won't have your night of passion ending in double pneumonia.'

Sara stiffened. Without a great deal of success she strove to disengage her hands. Ben chuckled and let her go, only to tuck one hand into the curve of his arm. With his free hand he brushed a lock of hair that had escaped back behind her ear and bent swiftly to kiss the place where it rested against her neck. Sara flinched. Seeing it, he frowned.

'What's wrong?'

'I—I'm cold,' she said lamely, obeying an instinct to hide her confused feelings. She was too responsive to him, too vulnerable. She withdrew her hand from his arm. 'And tired, too, after the flight, I expect. I'd better go to bed.'

Ben had noticed now. In the darkness, she could sense his puzzlement. He did not try to touch her again, but stood very still, looking down at her. It was too dark for him to make out her expression, but Sara bent her head involuntarily to escape those searching eyes.

'All right,' he said slowly. And then, on note of faint query, 'I'll make sure the windows are fastened against the storm and then join you.'

'No!' It ripped out of her like a cry of pain. She was backing away from him, making for the candlelit dining room, gabbling her excuses. 'No, I don't want you to. I wasn't thinking. I must be jet-lagged. 'I'm afraid I lost my head a bit,' she finished with an artificial laugh.

There was fraught silence. Then he said, 'For the second time.'

She was bewildered. 'Second time?'

'You said something along the same lines in Oxford, as I recall,' Ben said grimly, 'only then, I think you pleaded drink rather than jet lag.' He paused. 'What do you think you're doing, Sara?'

'I don't know,' she whispered wretchedly, unable to maintain her poise in the face of his scorn. 'But I didn't mean. . . .' She was unable to go on.

'That, at least, is obvious,' Ben said with bite. She saw him lift a hand and run it through his hair in an exasperated gesture. 'Oh, go to bed, Sara. Alone, if that's what you want. As you pointed out earlier in this delightful conversation, you have a right to your privacy.'

Another roll of thunder, much nearer this time, interrupted him. Great spots of rain spattered on to Sara's arm and she jumped, realising suddenly that her dress was still disarranged from his seeking hands. She pulled it straight, flushing in the darkness.

When the lightning came, she saw that he was looking at her under his brows sardonically. He seemed completely master of himself again, not even breathing fast, whereas she was shaking in every pore.

'I should stick to your privacy from now on,' he advised in a light, hard tone. 'The sort of game you play in company could get you into trouble.'

In the face of that mocking dismissal, she had nothing to say. She hesitated, cut to the quick by Ben's barely disguised contempt, but, before she could speak or make any other gesture, he had turned his back sharply and strode to the parapet.

Sara could bear no more. She fled.

CHAPTER FIVE

In her room Sara sank bonelessly on to the damask-covered stool in front of the mirror. The lamp on the dressing table lit her face with the cruel clarity of a make-up mirror light in the theatre. She was deathly pale.

Summoning up all her reserves of strength, she surveyed herself calmly. Her eyes were great emerald pools of hurt. It had been too dark for him to see her eyes, fortunately, because if he had, they would have given her away. They made her look like a child in pain who does not understand why.

She passed a shaking hand across her eyes. What was happening to her? After all the years of training, the determined discipline, she had lost all control over her body. Looking at the droop of the thin shoulders, the fluttering hands, in the mirror, she thought wryly that, if anything, her body was more expressive than when she had last danced. But it was utterly out of her power to command what it expressed. And all because—because of what? *Why* had this thing happened?

Sara leaned forward, inspecting her naked face with dispassion. Her mouth looked swollen. She ran her finger tips along her lower lip and found that it was tender. She supposed it was not surprising after that bruising kiss. Remembering it, she saw the blood come up under her pale skin.

She flung herself away from the mirror in an anguish of self-disgust. What was happening to her? Could she not even think about him without betraying herself?

Ah, but betraying what? The detached part of her brain asked. Betraying that for the first time in her life she wanted a man, this man, in a wholly adult fashion. And that she was too immature to handle it? Or was it something else?

Sara began to stride about the room in agitation, her knuckles pressed hard against her mouth. She had read about love at first sight, the divine madness that struck without warning but she had thought it was a fancy, a literary convention. She had danced the romantic solos with grace and precision but the feeling had all been as frothy as meringue. Could it be that she was wrong, that it was real and that she had now, in her turn, been transfixed by its terrible arrow? She had thought love was the stuff of dreams. That it belonged to heroines in books and the old poets. It could not touch sensible, hard-working Sara Thorn.

Her hair swung wildly as she shook her head, rejecting the idea. Ben Cavalli was not a man that one would fall in love with. At least, not if one had any sense of self-preservation. And anyway, she had been in love—with Robert—and it was nothing like this. She had wanted to be with Robert, to help him, to work with him. She had thought no further than that. But with Ben she was all sensation. Something in her cried out to him. He must know that.

She bit her lip, thinking exactly how much he must know of her reactions to him. He had proved it twice now. And he had had no doubt that he would be welcome in her room tonight.

Sara cast a nervous look at the door. Should she lock it? But no, he would not come now, he had made it very plain. Pressing her palms together with shuddering force, she knew that, in her secret heart, she wished he had not made it so plain. That he would ignore her resistance, overcome her scruples and immerse her in that passion that she knew she had only just held off this evening.

Her feelings appalled her. She was shameless. Ben

had not offered her a word of love; not so much as a casual endearment. And here she was agonising for him like a lovesick schoolgirl. How he would laugh if he knew. She could imagine the mockery those blue eyes would reflect if he ever found her out in her childishness.

Giving herself a mental shake, Sara picked up her little travelling alarm clock and began to wind it. It was late. She was tired. She was seeing everything out of perspective. One could not fall in love so rapidly—or so disastrously. The answer was probably simple: she had been too young, too preoccupied, to admit profound physical attraction to any man, up till now. There must be some sort of chemical affinity between herself and Ben Cavalli. He had unlocked all that previously unknown capacity. It was no more than that.

She would have to be careful not to let him suspect. Ben could break her if he ever found out how close she was to surrendering to his careless attraction. But if she were cautious, he need not know and then there would be no great harm done. She would have to make it plain, of course, that she was not here in the Palazzo as his plaything, no matter what his family retainers thought or he himself expected. It was more than flesh and blood could stand to have to hold him off, as she had done tonight, when every fibre of her flesh wanted him. But, provided she made her terms of reference clear, she did not think he would infringe on them.

Ben Cavalli, thought Sara desolately, setting down the clock on her bedside table, would not need to pursue reluctant secretaries. He was the sort of man who could attract any woman he wanted. He certainly attracted Daniella Vecellio and, from what she had seen, the feeling was mutual. Presumably, this evening's little interlude with herself was a casual thing, a way of passing the time in Daniella's absence. Her body burned with shame at the thought.

No, she told herself severely. You are being melodramatic. Put him out of your head. It will all look different in the morning. You will be able to deal with it in the morning.

It was a long time before she slept.

Sara dreaded meeting Ben again. She knew she would have to make it clear that there must be no repetition of last night, but did not know how she was going to do so without either giving herself away or rousing him to mockery. She approached the breakfast room next morning, therefore, with trepidation. It was unnecessary.

Only Uncle Luigi was there, eating apricots and drinking coffee the colour and consistency of black ink. He looked up from his newspaper and smiled when he saw her.

'I'm sorry. Am I late?' she asked noticing that another place had been laid and used at the far end of the table.

'Late? Of course not. We usually get up early here if we have work to do because it is so hot in the middle of the day that we just rest. Or at least, I do,' Uncle Luigi told her with a twinkle. 'When I'm writing I like to start at eight. But that doesn't mean you have to. And anyway, I don't think you should be doing any work today. You look peaky.'

Sara smiled. 'That's because I'm too pale and thin,' she told him calmly, helping herself to coffee. 'I'm quite tough really, though.'

Uncle Luigi pursed his lips. 'You always have shadows like sooty fingerprints under your eyes?' he asked politely.

She jumped. They were too observant, these Cavalli men. They took you unawares.

'I—I didn't sleep too well,' she confessed. 'It must have been the—the thunder. Or the strange surroundings.'

'Or something,' he agreed amused. 'Did you stay up late with Ben after I'd retired?'

Sara began to wonder if he were quite such a dear old man as she had thought.

'No, I didn't,' she said frostily. 'I was tired.'

'Ah,' Uncle Luigi looked more amused, 'that would account for it.'

Sara was suspicious. 'Account for what?'

'The fact that Ben was up so early,' he said innocently. 'First light, Guilio tells me. Been working like a demon since dawn. No doubt the result of his early night. Doesn't get a lot of early nights,' he added mischievously. 'I can see you're going to be a good influence on him.'

Sara was quite clear that she was being teased. That, too, seemed to be a Cavalli characteristic. So she choked down her indignation and said with monumental calm, 'I am not going to be any sort of influence at all on your nephew. For good or ill.'

Uncle Luigi looked unconvinced. She was not, however, to be drawn into the trap of protesting too much. So she allowed the silence to lengthen while she sipped her coffee.

Eventually, her companion said, 'I don't think I'm going to allow you to stay indoors today. You look as if you need a good dose of fresh air. We will start your sightseeing.'

Sara was startled. 'But I'm here to work,' she protested. 'I'm not a tourist.'

'Ben will be working all day,' mused Uncle Luigi as if he had not heard her. 'Salvatore will take us into the city. First of all, we will take you round the canals. Then we will walk a little. I shall enjoy myself. I haven't taken a delicious young woman round my city since I was a boy.'

Sara was taken aback by the gracefully casual compliment. It must have shown in her face because he smiled.

'You're a modest child, aren't you?'

She shook her head. The rapidity with which he and his nephew plunged into the most intimate conversations disconcerted her. She shook her head, dazed, and her lips twitched.

'I've never thought so,' she told him gravely.

'No.' He gave her a long, considering look. 'I can believe that. I can see now what Ben means.'

Her head reared up. Instantly alert, she felt her hand freeze on the cup she held. But she did not allow any of it to show in her calm face.

'What does Ben say, then?' she asked in a light, cool tone. She was very proud of it. It certainly seemed to deceive Uncle Luigi.

'Oh, it was just a casual remark,' he said absently, 'that you didn't seem to put much value on yourself.'

And that, she thought, burning with shame, was true enough. Though he would never know that it had never been true with anyone other than himself; that only he had the power of passion over her.

Her throat was suddenly dry. She swallowed hard.

'One values oneself differently at different times,' she remarked, as if they were having an academic discussion.

'Yes, that's true.' He smiled reminiscently. 'I thought I was a hell of a big shot when I was in the mountains. I was the only European for twenty days' march, and they treated me as an expert on everything from bow ties to electricity. Then, when I came home, I was nothing.'

The faintest bitterness was there that Sara had noticed before. She looked at him curiously, but forbore to question him. No doubt, if he wanted to confide, he would do so in his own good time. So she said no more, acquiescing in his plans to take her round Venice. She wondered briefly and uncomfortably what Ben would say when he found out that his uncle had been wasting time by taking the new secretary sightseeing, and decided that it was Uncle Luigi's problem to explain to his nephew. For her part, Sara was merely glad to have a reasonable excuse that would take her out of the house and away from the danger of bumping into him.

She did not, of course, confide any of her feelings to Uncle Luigi but she grew more and more suspicious that he was aware of them. There was that slight tone of amusement which he did not bother to hide whenever he spoke to her about his nephew or when Ben's name was mentioned, however fleetingly, in the conversation. Sara stalwartly ignored it.

In truth, it was not so hard to ignore Uncle Luigi's gentle teasing when they finally reached the city. After the thunder of last night, it looked as if it had been washed—no drenched—in light and air. Sara stopped in front of the great curlicued oddity that was St Mark's and sighed with pleasure.

'It looks,' she told her guide solemnly, 'more like a palace than a church.'

Uncle Luigi gave the great Basilica an affectionate but not uncritical glance.

'And so it is. A palace for St Mark. His body was stolen from Alexandria, you know, so they had to build him a suitable residence,' he matched her solemnity.

Sara laughed. 'I don't know about suitable. It's very opulent. Can we go inside?'

'Of course.' He looked at her sideways, consideringly. 'But wouldn't you rather leave it till—later, let us say. When Ben's less busy, he can bring you himself. Why don't we just wander round the streets today, so that you can get your bearings?'

Sara blushed and, furious, went on blushing. Uncle Luigi, greatly pleased, took her arm and led her round the Piazza, discoursing gently on the shops, the cafés, the people one met there, and what it had all been like forty years ago. She went unprotesting and, in the end, her blush died away. But she did not succeed in convincing him that she did not want to return to the city in his nephew's company.

They were walking along beside a small canal which glimmered in the morning sunshine when Sara saw some steps she thought she recognised. The last time she had seen them, they had been piled high with Daniella Vecellio's matched luggage. She hesitated, wondering whether to say as much to her companion. He paused, looking down at her.

'You must have come this way yesterday?'

She nodded. 'I—I think so, although, of course, so many of the streets look alike to me.'

'In time,' Uncle Luigi told her tranquilly, 'you will know every one like the rest of us.'

Sara let the implication of a shared future pass unchallenged. He gave a little sigh.

'That is where Mario Vecellio and his wife live. Mario used to own the whole Palazzo but the upkeep is ruinous and, anyway, he could not live in all of it. He and Daniella have no children.'

'She is very beautiful,' observed Sara in a neutral tone.

'Do you think so? She is not a type I admire,' the old man said with quiet finality. The subject of Signora Vecellio was obviously closed. He went on, however, to expound with enthusiasm on the date and history of the houses they passed, now mostly, to his regret, converted into apartments.

He clearly loved the city, and would have walked its streets and told its tales for hours. Nevertheless, as the sun grew higher and hotter, Sara could see that he was beginning to flag.

'Do you mind if we sit down?' she asked. 'It's all a bit too much for me: the sun and the buildings and the canals. Too much to take in at one go. You must remember, I'm only a cold little northern creature.'

Uncle Luigi flung back his head and roared with laughter.

'Cultural indigestion? By all means, let us find a café and survey the world from there. Provided you do not again speak of yourself so disrespectfully.'

Sara twinkled at him. 'It's the truth,' she protested.

He pinched her chin. 'If I were twenty years younger I would regard that as a challenge,' he told her. 'As it is——' a small, private smile curled his fine mouth, so like his nephew's that it was heartbreaking.

'As it is——?' she prompted.

The smile grew. 'As it is,' said Uncle Luigi outrageously, 'I shall hope to see you in good hands before you leave Venice.'

So, thought Sara grimly, there was little doubt as to Uncle Luigi's views. Any assault that Ben Cavalli might make on her peace of mind, not to mention her virtue, would have his uncle's wholehearted endorsement. No hope of an ally there.

Well, she would just have to make sure that Ben did not pursue his campaign any further on her own. She was not a child, and was, moreover, used to dealing with things on her own. There was nothing to get in a fuss about.

Except, said the small unwelcome inner voice, that she had never had to deal with Ben Cavalli before. She turned a deaf ear.

In fact, after their return from the city, Uncle Luigi announced that he was retiring to his room to rest, so there was little point in Sara staying indoors. Welcoming another respite, she changed into her old clothes and, after seeking directions from Salvatore, made her way to an isolated stretch of shore where the ducks waded and she could perform her prescribed ankle exercises unobserved.

She was concentrating hard on this when she heard her name called. She froze.

Looking up, she saw him strolling towards her. He was wearing stained jeans, a dark shirt with a patch of oil on the front and several buttons missing, so that it flapped open almost to the waist. He did not look like a respectable academic. He did not even look like the sophisticated man of the world that she had tangled with last night. In fact, he looked like nothing so much as a beachcomber and there was no reason why the sight of him should make Sara catch her breath and brace herself.

She stopped stretching her foot and pushed her hair back from her face with a hand that shook slightly. And waited for him.

'Salvatore said you had come this way,' Ben remarked, by way of greeting. 'How well did Uncle Luigi introduce our city?'

Sara smiled and a little of the tension went out of her. 'Beautifully.'

'Good. Do you think you will be happy here?'

'How could anyone not be?' she countered simply.

His mouth was wry. 'Very easily. You should hear my mother on the subject.'

He dropped on to a flat stone among the shale and patted the expanse beside him, mutely inviting her to join him. Sara looked quickly away to study the waving reeds. In this state of casual undress, he was more alarming than ever. She was bewildered by her own reactions.

'D-doesn't she like Venice?' she asked in a constricted tone.

Ben leant back on his hands and tilted his head to the sun. The long brown throat gleamed. Something in Sara faltered as if it had been challenged unexpectedly.

'Oh, my mother's too urban. She finds Venice provincial. Though she has fun playing house here on the island sometimes.' His voice was full of tolerant amusement. 'Do you like playing house, little Sara?'

'I've never had much opportunity,' she replied, trying to concentrate on what he was saying and not be distracted by those long beautiful hands or the strength of his shoulders under that apology for a shirt.

'No,' he said soberly at last. 'I don't suppose you have.' He squinted up at her. 'Uncle Luigi told me that you were without parents. I'm sorry. I hadn't realised.'

'Why should you?' she asked lightly. 'It's not something I bring up in casual conversation.'

'No,' he agreed. There was a good deal of meaning in his tone and Sara looked at him warily. But he was still basking there; he did not look angry; and when he spoke again his voice was smooth. 'Why did you tell Uncle Luigi?' he asked, not looking at her.

She had asked herself that question. It was not exactly a secret, but Sara was a private person and she did not normally make a present of such details to new acquaintances.

'I don't know,' she said at last. There was no mistaking the puzzlement in her. 'Perhaps I'd got to the point where I needed to talk. And, of course, he was perfectly charming.'

'Was he?' The brilliant eyes slanted swiftly upwards at that in a glance she could not interpret. 'I must ask him his secret.' He patted the stone beside him again, impatiently. 'For God's sake, sit down. I'll get a crick in my neck talking to you if you stay hovering like one of those silly birds,' he remarked, indicating with a disparaging arm the local seagulls.

She did as she was bid, tucking her toes out of sight under the full cotton skirt. It was not particularly old, but it had faded with much washing, and now looked as if it had very little more colour than the outcrop of rock on which they were sitting. She pulled it protectively round her legs and encountered a wry look from her companion.

'Suspicious of my intentions, Sara?' he mocked softly.

She felt the colour rise in her cheeks.

'Should I be?' she challenged.

He considered that. 'Oh, I think so,' he decided at last, a laugh in his voice.

She glared at him. 'Professor Cavalli——'

His brows came together in an immediate frown. 'Ben,' he rapped out.

Their eyes met, indignant green and combative blue and, in the end, it was Sara who gave way and lowered her eyelids.

'Very well,' she muttered. '"Ben", if you insist.'

'I do.' Now he had got his way, she thought resentfully, he was smiling again, letting that teasing caressing look come back into his eyes. She drew back from it, as from a palpable magnet.

'And you can say it again. Perhaps I should make you say it a hundred times, like they do to schoolchildren,' he mused.

Sara was outraged.

'I'm not a child.'

'No indeed,' he agreed, with an enthusiasm that brought the warmth to her cheeks. 'But you're not very old, either, are you? Or very sensible?'

Her spine stiff as a ramrod, she said with precision, 'I am quite sensible enough, thank you. I may not have hundreds of degrees but I run my life perfectly satisfactorily and without assistance.'

'Ah, that's the trouble,' he mourned. 'If you were *really* sensible, you'd reach out and take all the assistance that was available.'

Sara raised her eyebrows, in eloquent disbelief.

'If you reached in this direction, for example,' he prompted mischievously.

She looked at him for a long moment, at the laughing blue eyes and the torn ragamuffin shirt blowing in the evening breeze, and her mouth went dry at the thought of reaching for him. Her hand moved, flexed, almost as if she could feel that tanned skin under her fingers. She drew a shaky breath, turning her head so her hair hid her expression from him.

But he had seen that involuntary movement, heard her indrawn breath. Without any hurried movement he took her firmly by the shoulders and propelled her towards him across the sun-baked stone. Sara was assailed by a sharp stab of longing. If only she could reach out and touch him, in love, in confidence, how utterly willing she would be to go into his embrace and stay there. But she knew what he thought of her. And the iron clamp of shyness held her rigid.

Firmly, he turned her chin towards him, tilting her face so that he could look down into her eyes. Despairingly, she closed them.

'Don't do that,' said the soft, tantalising voice.

She shuddered, turning her head away the moment he released her chin. For a devastating moment she felt his mouth brush her cheekbone in the lightest of caresses. Not looking at him, she rushed into incoherent speech.

'Ben, I know you think I'm—well, I know I gave you every reason last night as well as that night in Oxford—but I'm not—it's not like that. Not for me. Normally.'

He was laughing. They were so close that she could feel the tremor of it in his bones, even though he made no sound. When he spoke, his lips moved against the skin of her temple.

'So, what is it like for you? Er—normally?'

Her precarious grip on her emotions was weakening. If only, she thought in panic, she could convince him that she was what Uncle Luigi had called a nice girl. Then he would realise that she was out of bounds, one of the people he despised, someone with whom he would not expect to play these sophisticated sensual games that, if she was not careful, would tear the heart out of her.

'I don't . . . I mean I'm not,' she began miserably, and was interrupted.

'You are delicious,' Ben informed her in a murmur, 'but you talk too much.'

One hand was at the back of her waist and now impelled her forward. Sara dragged hard against it, with a signal lack of success. He dropped his head to the curve of her shoulder where the old T-shirt slipped easily away before his questing mouth. His tongue traced gentle patterns on the warm skin of her shoulder. His mouth moved against her fragile collarbone until, with infinite gentleness, he came to the pulse in her throat where there was no disguising the disturbed beat of her blood. He paused, breathing fast, his eyes seeking her own in startled query.

Then, as if she had given him an answer, though Sara was positive she had neither moved nor uttered, he took her hard against him and his mouth found hers. There was no mischief in it now. All the laughter seemed to have been driven out of him, expelled by the force of a stronger element. Strained against him, Sara could not deny or refuse to recognise the hunger in him. She was frightened by it. But at the same time as she recoiled in alarm, she felt an identical hunger rising in herself. Her hands crept round him. In spite of herself, her mouth opened to his. The kiss grew savage with their fierce and mutual need.

It was he, finally, who broke it, and held her away from him. She could see that beneath the disreputable shirt his ribs were rising and falling like a runner's. But he was laughing again.

'Not only are you delicious. You are dynamite,' he told her, tucking a lock of hair behind her ear.

She put up a hand to smooth her hair and he caught it and carried it to his lips. He must have felt, as she did, that her hand was trembling convulsively against his mouth. She snatched it away, springing up from the rock.

Instantly, he was on his feet.

'No, don't be foolish and run off in panic,' he commanded in the soothing, reasonable sort of voice that he might have used to a frightened horse, she thought in disgust.

He possessed himself of her hands. She tugged uselessly at them, trying to drag herself away, but he would not let her go.

'Gently,' he rebuked her, still in that reasonable tone. A swift look told her that he was still amused. 'Or you'll tumble us both into the sea.'

'Let me go,' she begged in a breathless voice. 'Oh, *please* let me go.'

He gave her a little shake, not hard, and his hands slid warmly up her arms.

'I thought you weren't a child,' he mocked. 'You're behaving very childishly for a fully fledged adult.'

Sara had never felt less like an adult in her life. She was overwhelmed. She felt as cold and shivery as if she were ill and the echoes of that terrible need she had experienced at his touch were still reverberating. She felt bewildered and ashamed. And above all, she felt that she had to get away from this man who had, with a single wicked touch, shrivelled the veil of her ignorance to pieces and left her confronting the compulsions of her own nature.

'Leave me be,' she cried wildly.

His hands grew hard and hurting. The laugh disappeared from the blue eyes.

'Don't be a fool. You know what you want.'

She flinched from that as if he had struck her. His hands tightened.

'You can lie to yourself as much as you like, Sara Thorn, but don't try to lie to me. We had something terrific going for us, from the first time we touched, and not all your play acting can wipe it out. "I don't,"' he mimicked cruelly, '"I'm not" But by God, you are and you will.'

And after that, she was given no quarter. The former gentleness was banished along with his amusement. Her hands were imprisoned and her whole body hauled against his. She had never in her life felt so utterly in the power of someone else.

'Oh, please,' she moaned, 'please,' trying to free her hands, but he would have none of it.

He kissed her as she imagined he kissed the sophisticated ladies with whom he occasionally shared his life. Her very bones felt bruised at the impact of his hands, and his mouth on her skin was a kind of agony.

'Kiss me,' he muttered, against her lips as she tried vainly to turn her head away. 'Damn you, kiss me.'

But all she felt now was terror, the terror of any small, trapped creature that knows its only chance of survival lies in the faint possibility that its captor will be merciful. Her eyes, wide with the horror she was feeling, begged mutely for release. And, with a quick impatient sigh, he stepped back from her.

It happened so abruptly that she stumbled and had to put one hand out to the rock face to steady herself. She sank down on to the flat stone again. She was shaking badly.

She could not look at him but she knew with every fibre of her body that he was staring at her downbent head. Then, suddenly he shifted. Sara tensed instinctively. She could no more have prevented herself than she could have stopped herself shutting her eyes when she dived into a swimming pool. He noted it, frowning.

'Don't look like that,' he said roughly. 'I'm not going to hurt you. Good God, what do you think I am? Some sort of melodramatic adolescent—like yourself? But Guilio's coming. You'd better tidy yourself.'

She could not answer. She did what she could with her loosened hair. It was impossible to pin it up again, so she took off the little elastic circlet that had held it off her face and shook it free. Her T-shirt had been dragged off one shoulder, exposing a lacy strap and she pulled it back into place, blushing.

Ben said, 'Stop shaking. I've told you I won't hurt you.'

Sara raised her eyes then and he read disbelief in them. His brows snapped together.

'For God's sake. . . .' But Guilio was almost upon them. He hesitated, swearing under his breath, then he turned and ran lightly up the path to meet him. Sara could hear the rapid fire of question and answer. She turned her back to them and stared out to sea breathing carefully.

At length, he came back, moving so lightly over the shale she barely heard him. He touched her arm with an almost tentative hand. This time, she managed not to flinch.

'Look, Sara. I don't know what's wrong, but can't we talk about it?'

She turned to him.

'What is wrong,' she told him calmly, 'is your impression of me.'

'Oh?' He frowned. 'I would have said, on balance, that you were the more wrong about yourself,' he said 'I think I've got you pretty well assessed.'

That hurt. But she did not let it show. She shook her head.

'No, you haven't. You've caught me off balance a couple of times, that's all. And of course Dr Fredericks told you that silly remark I made about doing anything for money.'

His eyebrows rose. 'You mean it's not true?' he asked.

Sara swallowed. 'You know it's not.'

There was a little silence. 'Yes,' he agreed at last softly. 'I know it's not. I told you, I know you better than you think.'

She was startled. Her green eyes, wide and bewildered, sought his searchingly.

'The trouble is that everyone seems to have the idea that I am here as—as,' she hesitated, distracted with embarrassment.

'As what?' he asked, still softly.

She dared a quick look at his face, which was unreadable, and averted her eyes.

'As some sort of playmate for you,' she said brutally to the horizon.

There was a longer, nastier silence. Sara was prepared for mockery, for anger even, and this nerve-wracking silence frightened her. She clenched her hands till the nails were digging into the palms.

When he spoke, it was in a voice totally without expression.

'Do *you* think that?' It was the last thing she had expected him to say. The colour rushed to her face.

'No, of course not,' she gasped.

'Then—"everyone"—doesn't have that idea?' he mocked.

'Your uncle—he doesn't seem to expect me to do any work. Every time I suggest it, he says we must wait and see what you want me to do first,' she protested, stung into defending herself.

The lopsided smile grew.

'You must have realised by now that Uncle Luigi will do anything rather than settle down to work. I don't blame him. He's not as young as he was, and writing's a tough life at the best of times. But you will have to get him into the office not the other way round. I assure you, he's had no instructions from me to keep you at my disposal.'

It was the distaste in those last few words that finally convinced Sara.

'I—see,' she said with difficulty. 'I'm sorry. I thought——'

'It is,' said Ben Cavalli with evident fury, none the less intimidating for being icy, 'perfectly clear what you thought. I was perhaps partly to blame. Now that I understand the situation, however, you will have no further cause for complaint.'

He took her by the shoulders and gave her a brilliant smile that did not even attempt to reach his eyes.

'Don't start shaking again. I don't enjoy assault and battery. You are quite safe from my—attentions. We wouldn't want to give the servants or Uncle Luigi any encouragement in their gossip, would we?'

And he left her, dropping his hands from her shoulders with absolute finality and striding away up the path as if he were impatient to be done with her and get back to work.

Sara looked after him miserably. She was beginning to feel a fool and more than a fool. It was awful to have him speak to her in that clipped cold voice as if he could hardly bear to talk to her. And it was her own fault, too. Her own inexperience and the fiery longings he had unleashed in her had caused her to panic; lashing out, she had no doubt grossly over-reacted. She should have stayed cool, a little regretful, perhaps, and then they could still have been friends. As it was, she had blown it. He had sounded as if he would never speak to her again.

She did not see him at dinner nor at breakfast the next day. She was not sure whether or not that was a relief.

She did, however, determine the truth of his remark that Uncle Luigi would do anything to avoid settling down to work. After Sara had gently deflected suggestions of more sightseeing, swimming from the jetty or a tour of the Palazzo, Uncle Luigi was finally persuaded to enter the library which he used as an office and show her the manuscript on which she was to work. She felt compassion for him. Unable to ride or climb, he must now feel deprived. No matter how beautiful the Palazzo was, for a man used to the high, empty places of the world, it must indeed seem a prison.

So, to take his mind off his confinement, she told him something of her interlude with Ben.

'And I had to sit there and listen to his conversation with Guilio as if I were some sort of spy,' she ended miserably. 'There was no way I could get away from them.'

Uncle Luigi sympathised. 'To be an eavesdropper, this is unpleasant,' he agreed, adding mischievously, 'and it is so much worse when you cannot understand what is being said. I think you will have to learn Italian, little Sara.'

She laughed involuntarily. 'Uncle Luigi, you are outrageous,' she informed him, the last vestige of formality disappearing.

He appeared flattered. 'No, no. Merely practical.' He looked round the study. 'There must be phrasebooks here. Marianne did not speak a word of Italian when she was first married, and Marco had an absolute school of masters for her. Some of the textbooks are bound to be on the shelves if we look.'

'I'm here to work, not learn the language,' she protested.

'Then I shall tell Ben it is an *essential* part of your work,' said Uncle Luigi with resolution. 'After all, you will need to read my maps, won't you? and they are all in Italian. And at dinner we will speak only Italian.' He was highly delighted with his scheme. 'I shall tell Guilio to speak slowly and clearly. You will be fluent in no time. You will see. I am a very good teacher. My main talent was always for languages.'

Sara threw up a hand to halt his enthusiasm.

'Yours may be, but I'm by no means sure that I'm any good. And I'm sure that—er Ben,' she said his name with difficulty, 'would disapprove of us wasting the time he's paying for in Italian lessons for me.'

'Ben,' said Uncle Luigi unanswerably, 'is paying you for being here. When you work and what you do is entirely up to me. And *I* am determined that you shall learn Italian.

'You will find that it comes in very handy,' he assured her. 'In time.'

Sara regarded him suspiciously. 'Handy for what?'

Uncle Luigi allowed his eyes to crinkle up with laughter in a movement strongly reminiscent of one of his nephew's more wicked expressions, but his mouth stayed prim and his tone was innocent.

'Why, for eavesdropping, of course,' he said.

In view of this conversation, Sara was not surprised to receive a curt summons from her employer to see him in his study before dinner. It was delivered by Guilio, wearing an expression that Sara interpreted as one of silent sympathy though he was too discreet to be blatant about it. He presented Ben's note on an oval tray inlaid with slivers of pale wood which was probably she thought, hundreds of years old. The note, by contrast, was scribbled on a scrap of paper and signed with a great jagged signature as if he had been in too much hurry to do more than scrawl.

'Thank you,' she said to Guilio in a small voice. 'I'll go and see him as soon as I've changed.'

He looked grave. 'I think it would be best, signorina, if you went at once.'

Sara gave him a lopsided smile, 'I feel braver when I'm tidy,' she said ruefully.

Guilio bowed and turned away, leaving her to run up the staircase to her own room as fast as she could go. She showered rapidly and donned the same dress that she had worn to meet Uncle Luigi for the first time. Used to changing fast, in far less luxurious surroundings, she was ready in ten minutes, her hair shining and neat as a new pin, her face composed.

Ben's study was in the older wing, above the cellars and the cold paved hall that Guilio had told her had been the mediaeval armoury. It was reached by an ill-lit stone passage which had blatantly not yet seen the renovators' attentions. The door was heavy, unpolished oak, set in a massive stone arch, which could not be more different from the eighteenth-century elegancies of the main Palazzo. It was somehow typical of the man that he should choose such uncompromising surroundings.

Sara knocked timidly and such was the solidity of the door that she was afraid that she had not been heard.

She raised her hand to tap again, more forcefully, when the door was flung open and Ben himself appeared at it. Her hand was arrested in mid-flight and her mouth, as she afterwards thought in self-disgust, dropped foolishly open. For he had chosen to don dinner jacket for what, as Sara knew, was a simple family meal, and he looked, quite simply, magnificent. Sara, feeling more provincial than she had ever done in her life, swallowed hard.

'You're late,' he greeted her, looking her up and down with a cool expression that brought the blood running into her cheeks. 'Didn't Guilio tell you I wanted to see you at once?'

She said, with as much steadiness as she could muster, 'Yes, and I came as soon as I was ready.'

'That's put me in my place,' he observed. 'So now you have deigned to put in an appearance, will you come into my parlour?'

He stood back to allow her to precede him into his room, and she did so, a trifle hesitantly. That it was a work room was clear at first sight. The walls were covered in bookshelves and some sort of empty picture frame arrangement that looked, she thought confusedly, as if it might be a mechanical aid of some kind. There was a large drawing board, a visual display unit and three telephones. She also saw a machine with which she was more familiar—one of the most up-to-date dictation appliances.

There was also a desk, a scrubbed ash table with a pile of magazines and an Anglepoise lamp on it, and three worn leather arm chairs. He had obviously been sitting on one of these because its cushions were dented, there was an open file on the floor beside it, and an ashtray was balanced on its wide arm, bearing a half-smoked and still glowing cigarette. It was a wholly masculine room and, oddly, in spite of its slightly shabby, functional appearance, wholly personal as well.

Sara could imagine him here, studying the files in the pool of light from the lamp, alone late at night. Not for the first time, she wondered what it was that engaged so much of his attention. Was he another historian like Dr Fredericks? A linguist, like his uncle? He had never given so much as a hint. She would have to ask—but when he was in a friendly mood. Now, he was looking grim as she had never seen him. The fine mouth was compressed into a thin line.

'I gather,' he began slowly, 'that my uncle has not exactly—er—chained you to the typewriter since your arrival?'

'No,' Sara agreed with composure.

She sank into the chair next to the one he had vacated. He did not follow suit but went to the desk and perched on it, reaching behind him for a packet of cigarettes. Having extracted one, he lit it with absorption. Sara quietly leaned forward and stubbed out the cigarette still burning in the ashtray. He did not notice the movement, she thought.

'Did you not think that strange?'

She shrugged. 'Some people work like that—pootle about for ages and then fling themselves at work in a frenzy. I don't know your uncle well enough yet. . . .'

He gave her a long measuring look through the smoke of his cigarette.

'But you will, won't you? You are sparing no effort in getting to know him.'

Sara stared at him in bewilderment. 'Of course, he's my employer——'

She was interrupted. 'I'm your employer,' Ben said with deadly quietness. 'I found you. I brought you here. I pay your salary. Never forget that.'

She was half puzzled, half affronted.

'But I work for your uncle.'

Ben drew luxuriously on his cigarette. 'Do you? I would have said that's a moot point. I haven't seen much evidence of your work yet.'

It was so much what Sara had thought herself that she had no defence against it. She bit her lip.

'Since you are getting on so well together,' Ben went on smoothly, 'you will no doubt have gathered that Uncle Luigi, though a travelled and intelligent man, lacks—er—academic qualifications. This, in turn, has given him a quite unjustified sense of inferiority. Your role here——' he corrected himself '—your most important role here, is to see that he finishes the thesis that gets him that damned degree.'

She did not understand the angry sarcasm of his tone and shrank.

'I'll do anything I can. I like your Uncle Luigi; I want to help. . . .'

'Ah,' he mocked softly. 'Fortunate Uncle Luigi. His secretary will forego her sightseeing to perform the duties for which she is paid.'

'That wasn't my idea,' she protested, choked with the unfairness of it.

'No?' His eyes went over her in a cynical survey. 'Now, I would have said that you wanted to avoid me and had persuaded Uncle Luigi to assist you.'

Remembering her feelings when Uncle Luigi first

proposed the outing, Sara bit her lip, turning her head away.

'Yes,' he said. 'I thought so. Very dramatic.' In a sudden movement, he dropped beside her grinding out his cigarette in the ashtray and taking her chin between his fingers. 'Mary Queen of Scots, according to my uncle. Something to do with the collar, I suppose, and the hair—and those great tragic eyes.' A note, almost of pain, came into his voice. 'My uncle is very impressed by your air of tragedy. He is anxious that you shall not be made unhappy.'

'That is kind,' Sara said through stiff lips.

'I, however, am not kind,' Ben told her softly. He stood up. 'Whether you're happy here or not is entirely up to you. You will not, though, connive at Uncle Luigi's running away from his thesis. Or,' he gave her a small bitter smile, 'I will personally make your life hell.' His glance lingered on her lips. 'And I think you know that I could.'

CHAPTER SIX

THE evening had been one of the worst in her life, worse even than the days after Robert had decided he did not want to marry a crippled dancer. Guilio, or someone else, had clearly told Ben that she had been drinking cocktails with Uncle Luigi in the library, and Ben was furious. He barely spoke to her, and addressed his uncle in clipped tones.

Everything was made worse by the fact that they were not alone. When Ben finally allowed her to leave his study, Sara had fled as if from hell itself, only to discover in the black and white hall that Signora Vecellio had come to dinner. The lovely Daniella, in black silk and a pure white fox fur coat, looked perfectly poised against the marble balustrading. Round her throat was a diamond pendant, and she had falling diamonds in her ears that reminded Sara, a professional connoisseuse of paste jewellery, irresistably of miniature candelabra. But, however startling her appearance, Daniella was undeniably attractive. Ben had greeted her with considerably more warmth than he showed either of the chastened inmates of his house. During dinner, he devoted himself to her almost entirely, and afterwards escorted her to her home across the bay.

According to Uncle Luigi, he did not return that night.

Sara did everything she could to put Ben, and the unwelcome fascination he held for her, out of her mind. She worked passionately for Uncle Luigi, being often at her desk before seven. She exercised like a demon, either in the privacy of her room or else on the long unaccompanied walks she took on the island in the heat of the day.

When Uncle Luigi and all the staff were at rest, she would pull on an old skirt and shirt and betake herself to the far end of the island where there was a ruined chapel. On the shady sward in front of it, she would put herself through a gruelling routine with only an occasional surprised duck as audience.

Ben, contrary to everyone's expectations, had stayed on at the Palazzo. Neither she, nor his uncle saw much of him, but there were constant visits from Daniella Vecellio and, on the rare occasions that he left, it was always to visit her. Uncle Luigi muttered darkly and Sara, to her horror, found herself on the brink of real jealousy.

She knew she had no right to be jealous, that she was making herself ridiculous. She did her best to quell the feeling. She had been afraid of his intensity, of the warm laughter in his eyes; now that she was excluded from them, she realised wryly, she felt bleak indeed.

It did not help that she was not alone in her feelings. Simonetta, the plump kitchen maid, was boiling with rebellion and unrequited love. One morning, when Sara was accompanying Salvatore to Venice, they were joined in the launch by Simonetta whose virulent complaints proved an unwelcome test of Sara's improved Italian.

Eventually, Salvatore silenced her with one crisp phrase. As soon as the boat was tied up, Simonetta leaped out and disappeared into the crowd.

Salvatore shrugged philosophically.

'A bad case, that one. When she was little, the signore made much of her. Now it is different, and *la poverina* cannot understand why.'

He helped Sara out of the boat. She adjusted her shoulder bag, looking round.

'Why is it different now?' she asked, hoping the question sounded idle.

'She makes it very plain that she is not a little girl any more,' pointed out old Salvatore. 'So the signore stops playing with her. He is no fool, that one. And besides——' he hesitated, looking down at her, then succumbing to temptation, said in a rush, 'it is thought in the kitchen that the signore may think of marriage. Vittoria was speaking of it only this morning. It is after that that the little one was angry.'

Sara felt as if the ancient pavement had crumbled beneath her feet and desposited her in the cold waters of the canal. She stumbled, regaining her balance as Salvatore reached out a concerned hand to her elbow.

'M-married?' she croaked, not having, this time, to force a display of interest.

Salvatore cast her a curious glance. 'But yes, signorina. Before he went away, the signore said he had had enough of workmen and they were all to be out of the Palazzo before his return and not come back until the winter when he goes back to Boston. But now he has changed and the workmen are to come back this month. And they are to start with the apartments of the Count,' he added, referring by name to the principal suite of master bedroom and adjacent dressing and sitting rooms on the second floor. 'It was not originally intended that they should be redecorated for another year, but the signore himself has changed the plan.' He smiled. 'It is good that he is to marry. Those rooms have been empty since the Principessa left us.'

Sara swallowed, trying to endorse his enthusiasm. She knew that, at the moment, Ben slept in a room which she had never seen in the mediaeval wing.

'And do you—does Vittoria—know who he will marry?' she asked, trying to keep her voice indifferent. 'Signora Vicellio, perhaps?'

Salvatore was shocked. 'Oh no, signorina. Signor Vicellio is still alive; he is the signore's partner in business, you understand, though he is very much older than the signore. And even if the signora were free——' he shrugged, indicating with devastating clarity, that even if the lovely Daniella were free of the encumbrance of a husband, the signore would not marry her.

She was not, assumed Sara, the sort of woman the signore would marry. She was not, as Uncle Luigi had phrased it, a nice girl. Though she was no doubt a warm and willing partner in whatever relationship they had at the moment, she would not be an acceptable wife. Ben might behave—indeed would behave—as his fancy dictated, but his future wife would have to have an irreproachable past, thought Sara. She was submerging her pain in whipped-up tidal waves of indignation. Ben had had every intention of not marrying, according to his uncle, and she believed him. If, however, he decided to change his mind at this late stage, he would take a cynical heart and a good deal of dubiously achieved experience into a marriage. Nevertheless, he would, shamelessly, insist on impeccable innocence in his bride. Sara, by now in a fine fury, thought she was sorry for the bride.

She followed Salvatore round the fish market, taking little notice for once of the fish he chose and rejected. When he had finished and ordered the fishy parcels to be delivered later to their boat he turned to her apologetically.

'I have an appointment with the dentist, signorina. If you do not mind, I will leave you. Perhaps you will wait for me at the foot of Rialto, on this side at—half-past twelve?'

She nodded, relieved to be unexpectedly alone. With a friendly wave, he slipped away down a side street of the market.

Sara gave a long sigh, and began to stroll to the Rialto. There were shops there full of clothes and jewellery. She had marvelled at the elegance of the ware displayed there, and Daniella, to whom she had been speaking one dinner time, had looked pitying. The elegant shops in Venice, she was given to understand, were all around the Piazza. One only went to the Rialto when one was economising. Daniella, the implication was clear, never needed to economise.

To Sara even the shops on the Rialto had seemed expensive, though she had loved looking in their windows. She could not bear to eat into her hard-won savings to buy a dress or blouse which would wear out eventually, when the money could go instead towards healing her ankle. She knew, though, that her clothes which had never been of a class to stand comparison with Daniella's, had grown distinctly shabby during her stay. She had written to Sir Gerald, concluding gaily, 'But when I am a famous ballerina, I shall come back to Venice and buy myself a trunkful of wickedly expensive clothes.'

So now she made her way along the Rialto, window-shopping with enjoyment and no hint of discontent. She was peering into a jeweller's window, having pushed her sunglasses high on her head, to see better the glowing colours of his stones, when she felt a light touch on her arm. She turned, sighing, for it was not the first time an enthusiastic local had tried to pick her up. She met, to her utter surprise, the dancing blue eyes of her employer. He had not looked so friendly since the day of their arrival.

Sara gave him a hesitant smile in response. Ben came up to her side and looked in at the window she was contemplating.

'Trying to make up your mind to invest in a diamond bracelet?' he asked teasingly.

'I don't really like diamonds,' she said truthfully. They all looked like paste and diamante on the front of ballet costumes, she thought, but refrained from saying.

He raised his eyebrows. 'Then you're a most unusual female. What do you like in this window then?'

'The dragonfly,' she said without hesitation, pointing towards the little creature made of gold and chips of brilliant stones. 'I keep wondering what's in him. I can recognise sapphire and the amethyst, of course, but I keep wondering what that dark green is. It looks almost like marble.'

Ben peered at the dragonfly pin, balancing himself against the window with one hand. His bare forearm touched hers and she jumped as if singed by an electric current. He looked down at her wryly.

But all he said was, 'I should think it's either jade or one of the jade substitutes. It's not very expensive. Are you going to buy it?'

Sara shook her head. 'I've no money for luxuries.'

Immediately his brows drew together. 'We are not paying you enough?'

She could have cursed. Just when she thought she had steered clear of the trap, she had jumped straight into another. Now he would think she was complaining about the salary which, he must know, was very generous by any standard.

'No, no. It's just that I have other things to do with my money than buy pretty dragonflies.'

'What could be more important than buying a beautiful object?' he countered, lightly, though his eyes were oddly serious.

Sara bit her lip. 'Oh, lots of things, I should think. Security,' she swallowed hard, 'health.'

'And you think money can buy either?'

She raised her eyes to his face. 'Sometimes,' she said with a little difficulty, 'money can—help.'

He put a hand on her shoulder.

'Any security that you can buy with money,' Ben said very deliberately, 'is no security at all. In the end, the only thing we have to rely on is our fellow men—their good will, their good faith. You can't buy either.'

For a moment, Sara stood very still. It sounded as if

he meant it. More, it sounded as if he wanted her to believe it, as if, however fleetingly, he cared enough to reach out to her. It thawed out her heart a little. She found herself smiling at him shyly.

'I know that's true in general,' she admitted, 'but sometimes particular circumstances . . .' She could not go on.

Very gently, as if he were afraid of frightening her, Ben took her arm and looped it through his own, folding his right hand over her own resting just above his left elbow. Then he began to urge her along the bridge, past the shops that she had looked at earlier.

'And your circumstances are so particular?' Ben queried softly.

Sara hesitated. The seductive voice was almost irresistible, but if she once told him what he wanted to know she was very much afraid she would be in his power for ever.

'Look,' she hedged desperately, 'we got off on the wrong foot but. . . .'

'On the contrary,' he said, his voice full of amusement, 'I would say we got off very much on the right foot.' He stopped and she perforce halted too. He looked at her very steadily, his mouth curling with that private laughter that she was so wary of. 'It was only later that we—er—got out of step. When you decided to start holding out on me.'

She turned her head sharply.

'I don't know what you mean.'

'Yes, you do,' Ben said calmly, 'but if you like, we can go and have a coffee, and I can explain all over again.'

That instantly threw her into confusion.

'Oh no, I have to meet Salvatore any moment now. He's been to the dentist but I promised I'd wait for him and be ready to go back when he'd finished.'

'Salvatore,' said Ben with the faintest hint of

annoyance, 'can go back on his own. We'll go and tell him.'

Sara still hesitated. She was as eager as a schoolgirl to spend the day with him, she thought ruefully. But long term, would it not make it all the harder to bear? Would it not be easier to forget if she saw as little of him as possible? Because she would need to forget him when she was home again. When—she said to herself deliberately—he was married.

Ben, perhaps fortunately, did not wait for her decision. He seemed to know where Salvatore had moored the boat—presumably, it was his normal practice to leave it at just that station—and he marched off the Rialto and round to the boat at some speed. Salvatore was promptly despatched to the island with the equivocal message that Ben would look after Signorina Sara for the rest of the day and bring her home safely for supper. And then—without Simonetta who had not returned to the boat—Salvatore departed for the open lagoon.

'Right,' said Ben with decision. 'The Piazza. And thereafter, whatever sights you have not managed to see already. And, of course, shopping.'

Sara laughed, shaking her head. 'You haven't been listening to me. No shopping.'

He gave her a cool appraisal. 'None at all? I can appreciate you may not feel you can afford dragon-flies, but surely a new—er—blouse would not come amiss?'

Sara looked down at the T-shirt. It was washed out and thin in places, but surely it was still respectable?

'Am I not decent?' she asked anxiously.

'You,' Ben said crushingly, 'look like a downtrodden skivvy. You're as skinny as a scarecrow and it won't be long before you fall through your clothes—and that goes for your shoes as well.'

'You,' she returned sweetly, 'would do better to mind

your own damned business. You don't own me. I work for you.'

'I'm glad you've not forgotten it,' he told her. 'It will make you see why I'm not prepared to trot you round Venice—which is after all my home—looking like a half-starved slave. If you won't think of your own reputation, at least spare a thought for mine.'

'Are you suggesting I go buying large amounts of clothes that I don't want and don't need, just so that your friends can think what a munificent employer you are?' she demanded, shaking with rage.

'Yes,' he said promptly.

She stopped dead. 'How dare you?'

There was a distinct gleam in the blue eyes. He did not, however, answer fire with fire but took her arm peaceably and steered her out of the way of a woman laden with flowers.

'Only I, of course, shall make myself responsible for the bill,' Ben said smoothly. 'As it is at my behest that you are doing it.'

There was a silence while Sara digested this and they walked on. He appeared to have put the whole thing out of his mind, having settled it to his satisfaction, and looked about him with pleasure. Sara, however, was not so easily convinced.

'I can't have you buy me clothes,' she protested at last.

'You can either come with me and choose what you like,' he said with great firmness, 'or you can sit in a café and I will go to every dress shop round the Piazza, explain exactly who you are and what you look like to the manageress, and buy whatever she recommends. Take your choice.'

Sara stared at him. 'But good heavens—wouldn't that cause you a lot of gossip?'

'A veritable flood,' he said smugly. 'If you don't like gossip, I'd advise you to co-operate.'

Dazed, she shook her head. 'But I thought the object of the exercise was to avoid gossip.'

'There is,' observed Ben unanswerably, 'gossip and gossip.'

Sara was suspicious. 'What does that mean?'

'It means that I am perfectly prepared to be talked about for having been on a spree buying clothes for my uncle's beautiful secretary,' he told her teasingly, 'I am not prepared to be known as the man who keeps beautiful girls shut away on his island and dresses them in rags. It is,' he explained with a blandness that made Sara want to hit him, 'a question of image.'

'If you insist,' she said at last stiffly.

'I do.' He stopped and pinched her chin between his thumb and forefinger. 'Don't look so tragic,' he mocked. 'It's fun buying new clothes. Or so my girlfriends tell me.'

The mention of his girlfriends made her retreat even more.

'Whatever you say,' she said.

'Oh, you're such a prickly little creature. We'll have some coffee first to strengthen you for your ordeal,' he explained mischievously, 'and then we'll look at the shops. And if you don't say "thank you" nicely at the end of the day, I shall take strong steps.'

An unwilling smile was dragged out of her.

'I think you're mad,' she sighed.

But she went with him.

It was a memorable day. Sara managed to confine Ben's generosity to the extent of accepting no more than a plain skirt and a couple of elegant and wickedly expensive blouses from him. She bought a pair of dainty strapped kid sandals for herself. And absolutely and finally refused to accept a cocktail dress of bronze velvet with collar of old cream lace. They had a considerable altercation about it, to the amusement of the shop assistants. It was only when Sara threatened to tip all his previous purchases out of their discreet carrier bags on to the grey-carpeted floor of the salon that Ben finally acquiesced. But it did not leave him in a good temper and he was muttering direfully to the manageress as he paid for a forest green silk shirt. In spite of having lost what must have been a substantial sale, the manageress was all sympathy for Sara and cordiality itself as she showed them out of the shop.

'Right,' said Ben. 'Now we take a gondola and do the tourist circuit. And if'—he added with a baleful look—'you dare to quibble about who pays for it, I shall tip you into the canal and leave you there.'

'Yes, sir,' said Sara meekly. She judged it best to antagonise him no further and added in a placatory tone, 'I am really very grateful for your generosity.'

He stopped dead on the way to the canal and threw back his head in a paroxysm of laughter. When he could speak again he said, the mirth still bubbling in his voice, 'Sara Thorn, you are an abominable liar. You are not in the least grateful, and thank God for it.' He tucked the packages under one arm and took her hand with his free hand. 'I don't want you grateful. Remember that.'

She was puzzled. But there was no point in questioning him further. For one thing, he was bustling her into a gondola, pointing out places of interest, persuading the grinning gondolier, whom he seemed to know, to sing in a cracked voice. For another, she had the distinct impression that he had given more away than he was quite prepared for, and did not intend to be drawn further. So she settled down happily to see Venice the traditional way.

It was not, in the end, as romantic as might have been expected. They were lovely canals, of course, and some of them were quiet enough, but on the main thoroughfares, their light craft was constantly assaulted by waves from motorboats and vaporetti, the local water buses. Once or twice, she was alarmed at the rocking of the boat in the wake of some fast machine. Once she reached for the edge of her seat to right herself, and found her fingers caught and held in a firm clasp for the rest of the journey. She did try to ease them free, turning reproachful eyes on her companion, but he had smiled blandly and refused.

CHAPTER SEVEN

It was just as well that the household did not know that the signore had held her hand throughout their sightseeing trip. It had been news enough that he had sent Salvatore home alone. Even Guilio had been unable to suppress a certain dignified speculation when he greeted Sara on her return. And Uncle Luigi was downright gleeful.

'That,' he told Sara with relish, 'will be one in the eye for Her.'

She knew him well enough by now to recognise that he spoke of Signora Vecellio. The lovely Daniella made no secret of the fact that she found Uncle Luigi's presence in the Palazzo an intrusion and his companionship at her dinners with Ben an irritant. Uncle Luigi disliked her cordially and spared no opportunity to make it plain. Daniella, however, being used only to admiration from the male sex, appeared not to be aware of Uncle Luigi's barbed remarks.

Now Sara said defensively, 'I don't see why.'

'Don't you?' Uncle Luigi fitted a cigarette into his holder with elaborate care. He did not usually smoke in the library where fire was a distinct hazard to the collection of books, and Sara interpreted this move as an indication that he was preoccupied.

'I do not, of course,' he went on carefully, 'know what Ben gets up to when he is away. The gossips say—but then it is a mistake to listen to gossips: they usually get things wrong. But here, at least, he is utterly anti-social. He works—amazingly hard. For recreation, he sails, he swims, he reads. But he does not invite girls to accompany him here, and he does not go into Venice to visit any. At least, not that I know of.'

'But he goes to visit Signora Vecellio,' pointed out Sara, depositing the papers on the desk and removing the pile from Uncle Luigi's elbow out of harm's way.

'Daniella, yes.' Uncle Luigi stared at the ceiling, musing. 'That I don't understand. Her husband, Mario, is an old friend of the family. He is a lot older than she is, you see. In age, Mario must be somewhere between Ben and myself. He was always very good to Ben as a schoolboy. Mario was very busy, very dedicated. We never thought he would marry. Then, two or three years ago, he comes back with Daniella.'

Sara shuffled the papers, righting them. She looked absorbed in her task. Uncle Luigi observed her downbent head with a good deal of compassion.

'I always thought Mario and Daniella were quite devoted,' he said, his doubtful tone at variance with the words. 'In spite of the age difference.'

Sara looked up and gave him a swift, unhappy smile. 'I have never met her husband.'

'No. Well. He is busy. He cannot come to Venice whenever he wants. He has his responsibilities. And while Ben. . . .' He broke off, shrugging.

But Sara knew what he was going to say. Mario Vecellio was Ben's business partner. As long as he was out of Venice, Ben had a clear field with his lovely wife in her lonely apartment. It hurt. It hurt surprisingly badly.

She bit her lip. Were they having an affair because Daniella was bored and lonely? And Ben? She shied away from the thought. She did not know Ben well enough to speculate why he might want an affair with his friend's wife. Or indeed why he might have wanted an affair with his uncle's secretary. But there had been no doubt that it was in his mind when he brought her to Venice. And she had been too blind to see it, though even the servants had come to the right conclusion.

It occurred to her suddenly that the absent Mario might be willing to divorce his wife. If he did, if perhaps he was already in the process of doing so, Daniella might be the unnamed lady that the hated Ben was thinking of marrying.

Sara sat down abruptly. Uncle Luigi, still ruminating, did not notice.

'She must have known when she married him that Mario was devoted to his work. And she has everything she asks for—servants, lots of clothes, jewellery; the freedom to do whatever she wants.'

'Perhaps she wants things she doesn't ask for,' said Sara, overcoming a constriction in her throat.

He narrowed his eyes against the smoke of his cigarette, 'Personally, I think Mario is a fool. And as for Ben—I just don't understand his part in it at all. It is utterly unlike him.'

'Perhaps he is in love with her,' said the expressionless little voice.

Uncle Luigi snorted, putting one hand over her two which were plucking at the corners of the papers she had retrieved. He held them firmly in a comforting clasp.

'That one,' said his fond uncle with concentrated fury, 'has never been in love in his life.'

So she knew. His uncle, whose affection for him was undoubted, confirmed her own suspicion. Ben was a highly attractive man who could, without very much effort on his own part, acquire whatever sexual satisfaction he might from time to time decide that he wanted. She could congratulate herself that he had not wanted her very much or she could have been in for a bad time of it.

As it was, he left her alone. Sara found it a relief, or thought she did. In the long, hot Venetian nights while the birds wheeled, calling outside her window, she told herself how lucky she was. The work was interesting, Uncle Luigi was the friendliest of employers, Venice itself an enchantment. For the first time for years, she was free, independent, her anxieties shed in the sheer interest of her daily round. She did not waste a thought on Robert; she had not forgotten him, but he seemed like a figure in a play, not quite real any more. And all the time she grew stronger, happier, her self-confidence returning.

Meanwhile, the book was proceeding well. Now that the end was in sight, Uncle Luigi had abandoned his rest after lunch. Indeed, he could hardly bear to eat at midday, and nearly always ended up by urging Sara to bring her coffee back into the library so they could carry on. Conversation at dinner, at which Ben now generally joined them, was wholly about the map collection. Daniella, whose visits seemed to have decreased, looked heartily bored.

On one such occasion, Daniella took the opportunity to take Sara aside while uncle and nephew were in the library scanning a parchment scroll under a microscope.

It was a warm evening and Guilio had set nuts and olives and a large jug of some concoction of his own on the wooden table on the terrace. A couple of stout candles in flower-pots illuminated the table and there was a stand with a brazier burning in it at the edge of the terrace. Daniella, in floating voile and a dramatic Spanish shawl, looked suitably exotic.

'How lovely it is here,' Daniella remarked, letting the shawl fall on to the dusty paving. Sara picked it up. 'I always tell Ben that he should move the kitchen and turn the kitchen and breakfast room into one long drawing room overlooking the sea. It is such a waste to leave this view to the servants.'

'The servants are here all the year round,' pointed out Sara with justice, 'and Ben never uses the drawing room anyway. I don't see that it's a waste.'

Daniella was not best pleased. 'Ben has not used the drawing room up to now. But his habits could change.'

'Could they?' Sara was wide-eyed. Fairly certain that the Italian girl was out to make mischief, she was determined to be as unco-operative as possible. 'Why do you say that? He seems pretty set in his ways to me,' she added with some dryness.

Daniella's foot, in orchid pink kid, began to tap bad-temperedly on the cross-bar of the table.

'Of course, he would do so, since you have known him such a little time,' she said. She bent her head to examine her lacquered nails in the flickering candlelight. 'But to those of us who know him well, Ben has changed considerably in the last months.'

Sara helped herself to an olive, resisting an unladylike temptation to bat it hard in the direction of one of Signora Vecellio's eloquent brown eyes. With her mouth full, it would obviously be rude to respond to Daniella's remark. So, to that lady's frustration, Sara chewed her olive and vouchsafed no response.

'He is,' pursued Daniella in a steely voice, 'becoming clear at last about what he wants.'

Sara took her time about her olive and then said casually, 'He's always given me the impression of knowing exactly what he wants.'

Especially, she thought silently, when it has happened to be me. Not too many doubts there, as I recall.

Daniella gave her a smile like a stiletto. 'Naturally, Ben does not wear his heart on his sleeve.'

'Oh, we're talking about his heart, are we?' said Sara with a cheerfulness that clearly succeeded in its object of reducing Daniella Vecellio to frustrated fury. 'Well, I can't give you any opinion on that, signora. In fact, it's news to me that he has a heart.'

And that, she thought vengefully, ought to shut her up. She was shaking herself with anger at Daniella's impertinence. Really, she could not begin to understand how Ben could waste his time with such a vulgar, malicious woman. She stood up, preparing to go in search of the men to relieve her of the burden of the undiluted company of their guest, only to find herself forestalled.

Uncle Luigi came forward from the French window to take Daniella's hand. Behind him, half in shadow, stood Ben.

He must have heard. Sara, frozen with horror, realised that there was no way he could have avoided overhearing that last remark of hers. And, of course, he would not realise that it was said to spite Daniella. He would take it as a deliberate and calculated insult. She swallowed. Her eyes, clearly illuminated by the candles, held an expression half-placatory, half-defiant.

Ben strolled forward, his mouth wry. He looked, Sara thought, more rueful than angry. She expelled a long breath of relief.

All he said was, 'Has Daniella given you your post?'

'No,' she said in surprise.

'She was kind enough to pick it up for us at the main post office. In fact, if she had not decided to come on an errand of mercy and deliver it in person, we would not have had the pleasure of her company tonight,' Uncle Luigi said sweetly.

Sara resisted the urge to giggle. Uncle Luigi could not have said more plainly that Daniella had used the letters as an excuse to ask herself to dinner. But Daniella did not notice, preening at what she had understood as a tribute to her generosity. How *could* Ben, thought Sara in exasperation: vulgar, malicious and stupid as well. She would bore him in a week, surely?

But Ben was frowning, brushing his uncle aside, setting himself to be pleasant to Daniella. Balked, Uncle Luigi turned his attention to the jug on the table.

It was filled with a liquid the colour of dragon's blood. It had a central funnel full of ice which thus kept the drink cool without diluting the alcohol. Sara admired the jug as Uncle Luigi poured and handed to her a small measure of the drink.

'A design of my own,' he said airily. 'Saw a lot of things like that in the mountains. I just adapted it and had a friend make it for me.'

Sara was impressed, and said so. 'But isn't glass terribly difficult to make?'

'It takes a lifetime to learn how to do it properly,' Uncle Luigi agreed, 'but the simpler pieces are just a matter of practice. Have you never seen it done?'

'Never,' she confessed.

'Then, while you are here, we must take you to Murano. There has been glass-blowing there for centuries.'

She was intrigued. 'Where?'

'Murano,' said Ben, who had clearly been listening to their conversation with one ear, 'is another island in the lagoon. Rather larger than this one, I may say. Well, it's five little islands really. It used to be the place where all the mirrors in the world were made. It was forbidden to export the secret of how it was done. Nowadays, they make mostly decorative glass. It's a bit of a tourist trap. The quality is very uneven. But if you go to one of the older men, like Uncle Luigi's friend, you can see some good work. I'll certainly take you if you'd like to see it.'

Daniella intervened. 'Do not embarrrass Sara, darling. She would be ashamed to drag you away from your work just to act as a guide. She can quite well go on one of the tourist excursions.'

Uncle Luigi interrupted before Ben or Sara could reply.

'Do have some of this, Daniella. Guilio has become quite an expert in cocktails and this is a creation of his own.'

'Yes, indeed, we must not disappoint him,' she said graciously. 'He told me when I arrived, that he had thought up something new and was naming it after me.'

Ben laughed. 'Then we shall undoubtedly soon be asking for glasses of Daniella in all the smart bars of the city. Immortality at last, my sweet,' he teased, raising his glass in a silent toast.

'Oh, it's not called Daniella,' Uncle Luigi protested. 'The name will generally give you some idea of what's in it. Anything called "Lady", for example, usually includes gin and fruit juice.'

Sara sipped hers experimentally, tasting orange and, she thought, peach juice.

'And this?'

Uncle Luigi pondered. 'I am not sure in English.' He looked under his lashes at Daniella. 'Disastrous Lady?' he mused.

'Dangerous Lady,' snapped Daniella.

'Ah yes, of course, how silly of me.' He smiled at her charmingly. 'But at my age, you know, one forgets the simplest things.'

Sara, who did not for a moment believe in the sudden diminution in the standard of Uncle Luigi's English, said hastily, 'Well, it's certainly delicious. I shall tell Guilio so.'

Uncle Luigi gave her his hand. 'Let us go and do so at once. And then——' he smiled at Ben, '—perhaps you will bring the Disastrous Lady to table.' He paused and then concluded deliberately, 'Along with Daniella, of course.'

'That,' said Sara, when they were inside, 'was not very kind.'

'Possibly,' said Uncle Luigi, unrepentant. 'But it was amusing.'

For some inexplicable reason, Sara found that his glee at discomfiting their guest was balm to her sore heart. She did not want to examine why her heart was sore in the first place, and her ungenerous reaction made her ashamed.

She sighed and he looked at her incredulously.

'Oh come along, my dear. That woman has the hide of an elephant. She won't have noticed or minded anything.'

Sara smiled but bit her lip. 'Ben will, though,' she said unhappily.

'That,' said Uncle Luigi, squeezing her hand, 'is Ben's look out. If he is really stupid enough to— Oh, I have no patience with him. I'll tell Vittoria we're ready to eat now.'

He stamped off to the kitchen, clearly out of temper. Sara stared after him with a faint frown. Had Uncle Luigi too come to the same conclusion as was beginning to force itself upon her—that Ben was eventually intending to marry his partner's wife? Uncle Luigi would be upset. He did not like Daniella. Even more, he disliked Ben deceiving his partner and taking advantage of the man's absence. Uncle Luigi's affection for his nephew was compounded with respect, but he was not blind. And he could not bear Ben to behave in a way that fell short of his own standard.

Well, Uncle Luigi was old fashioned, Sara thought a little bitterly. Ben seemed to have little compunction for the way he was acting with Daniella and, as for Daniella herself, she positively gloried in it.

During dinner, Sara watched them covertly, hardly able to tear her eyes away. Daniella was full of some party or other that they had been to. It was obvious that the main reason for her describing it in such detail was to make it plain to her auditors not only that she had been the most admired woman present, but that Ben Cavalli had not left her side all evening. Uncle Luigi greeted this monologue in furious silence.

Sara thought she had never seen Daniella so self-assured, so wholly possessive of Ben. She kept laying her hands on his face, his arm, so that the long, painted nails showed up against his skin like patches of blood. Sara shuddered, looking away.

She was more than half certain that Daniella would not return to Venice tonight. She could imagine them going off to Ben's room with their coffee and brandy, playing soft insidious music on the stereo while

Daniella touched him with those elegant predator's hands. And then, because she was beautiful, and clearly available, Ben would urge her to stay with him, and she would do so.

Sara swallowed. The evil taste in her mouth was a physical reality. She told herself she did not understand it. Ben Cavalli, thank God, was no concern of hers. Since she herself had turned down the chance to spend the hours of night in his arms, it should not bother her who shared his bed.

She came back to the conversation with a start, finding herself addressed by Ben, his eyes compelling.

'You're not going to bed yet, are you?'

Still dazed, she shook her head. Looking round the table, she realised that the coffee was drunk, the meal finished. Uncle Luigi was at the door saying goodnight and Daniella Vecellio, her gypsy scarf wound peasant fashion round her head and shoulders, was offering a chilly farewell.

'N-no. I want to read the letters Signora Vecellio brought,' she said.

'Good. Wait for me in the library. I won't be long.'

It was said so softly Daniella could not possibly have heard. Sara's eyes widened. He had turned on his heel and was ushering her out, a rubber-encased torch in his hand. As Uncle Luigi left, Sara went to the window to watch the light of Ben's torch bobbing down the path to the landing stage. Her heart beat heavily so that it was almost a pain under her ribs.

Desperately, she fled to the library, opening her letters at random. The first was from Sir Gerald. She would be glad to know that the season was profitable. Rehearsals started in September. He was keeping a place for her, assuming that Dermott Andrews' miracle cure would work. He was glad to hear that she was so much more cheerful and like herself again, and was looking forward to hearing all her news. The last three words were heavily underlined. There was also a scrawled postscript: Sir Gerald hoped that she had sent that young bounder Ericsson about his business.

Sara looked down at her ankle and flexed it thoughtfully. It was undoubtedly a good deal stronger already than she had ever hoped it could be. She had written to Mr Andrews to tell him that she not only had enough money but also felt sufficiently fit to undergo the course of treatment he had recommended now. He had not yet replied, but Sara expected, from his previous letters, that he would find it easy enough to get her into the clinic at Como.

Four months ago, she would have been desperately excited at the thought. Now, it was tainted with the reflection that, when she went off to Como, she would probably never see Ben again. Unless he liked the ballet, of course. But he had never given any sign of it. He was fond of music. She had heard him playing it by the hour. But, in all the time she had lived in his home, she had never once known him go to the opera or ballet. So, in all probability, when she left the Palazzo, she would leave him for good.

She tried to look on it as a step forward, a step towards forgetting his powerful attraction. But, just at the moment, waiting for him to come back up that midnight stair, she could not.

She heard the door open behind her. Ben's voice with an unmistakable hint of laughter said, 'Has some kind neighbour forwarded your gas bill?'

She turned slowly and smiled with an effort.

'Does it look like it, then?'

He shut the door softly behind him and came across to her. Oh God, she would know that graceful, loping stride anywhere, and she would know it for the rest of her life.

'You were looking moderately tragic,' Ben told her lightly. 'You have the most expressive back, did you know that?'

A dancer had to express emotion with her whole body, of course, but he did not know she was a dancer, and it was far too late to tell him now. Now that she would soon be gone.

He might have laughed. She had expected him to laugh, to tease her and then to continue the conversation in the bantering style he now normally adopted with her. But he did not. Instead, he looked at her searchingly. She answered with a touch of constraint therefore.

'And my back said "gas bills"?'

He might have laughed. She had expected him to laugh, to tease her and then to continue the conversation in the bantering style he now normally adopted with her. But he did not. Instead, he looked at her searchingly.

'Perhaps not quite. But something unwelcome. Have you had bad news, Sara?'

Utterly overset by his concern, she could do no more than shake her head.

'Then, what is it?'

But she could not answer that either. After a pause, he turned away and flung himself down on a battered chaise longue under the window. He looked sensuous.

'Sara, ever since we met, I've had this feeling that you have been desperately unhappy. As if you have been carrying something which is more than you can bear. Was I wrong?'

The red head dipped, sank.

'No,' she said, in a small voice.

'You——' It was an exasperated sound, bitten off almost at once. As if with a great effort, he resumed in a gentle voice, 'I know you were—disconcerted about what happened when we first met. You made that,' a certain dryness invaded his voice, 'very clear. Have you been torturing yourself because of your absurd conscience about that night?'

Startled, she looked up, and their eyes locked.

'So.' Ben expelled a long breath. 'It's not misplaced remorse. Thank God for that, at least. I thought I had gone beyond the pale.'

'But it was me,' Sara gasped, uncomprehending. 'You were so angry with me for the way I behaved. You said so.'

Ben's smile was a little twisted. 'My dear child, don't you recognise frustration when you see it? Not to mention jealousy?'

'Jealousy?' Sara was incredulous.

'The intrusive fiancé,' pointed out Ben, with something of a snap, 'in his time had presumably got further than I had.'

'Oh.' She looked away, wishing that she did not blush so easily or that he would not lounge there, looking so handsome. The elegant bone structure of his face, the midnight hair, the cool, hard mouth that sometimes wasn't cool and hard at all, all made her melt with the desire to touch.

'Only, you weren't telling about him,' Ben went on. 'You still aren't. Is he the one that makes you look so sad?'

Sara swallowed. 'I didn't know that I looked sad. I have no cause. I've been very happy here. You're all so kind. And I love your Uncle Luigi.'

'Lucky Uncle Luigi.' Ben was dry. 'So you're as happy as a bug in a rug? All right. I'll buy that. You're happy sometimes.' His voice softened. 'When you're on your own, by the chapel.'

Sara froze. 'You've *seen* me?'

'I have watched every move you make,' Ben told her coolly.

'You've spied on me! How could you? I didn't know. . . .'

His eyes swept up and held hers so that she stopped in the middle of her distress, shocked by what she saw on his face.

'I had to. You wouldn't talk to me. Wouldn't let me get near you. What else was left to me but to watch you?'

'I—I don't understand,' she faltered.

'Don't you?' He was bitter. 'Well no, perhaps you don't at that.' He gave her a lopsided smile. 'Well, I'll explain it to you. The truth, little Sara, is that I have wanted you, quite desperately, from the first time I saw you standing on the stairs in that flaming velvet in Oxford.'

She made a small, inarticulate protest, her hands flying to her cheeks in consternation.

'Only I haven't had you.' Ben went on remorselessly. 'And for a man of my temperament—who usually takes what he wants and quickly—that was——' he paused, regarding her steadily, 'unacceptable.'

Sara gave a hard little laugh. Unacceptable! As if she were the subject of some sort of sordid business agreement.

'Tough,' she said between her teeth, distress drowned in a flood of indignation.

He laughed at that, softly. 'Oh, it was. I don't think you can imagine how tough. You're not much given to the needs of the flesh yourself, are you? In spite of that body—and it speaks like a second voice, you know that, don't you—in spite of the way you look, you're a pretty frigid little article at heart.'

Sara was icy with outrage. 'How dare you!' she hissed.

He gave her that lopsided smile which did not reach his eyes.

'Frigid,' he murmured. 'And not very original either.'

Sara was not so angry that she did not recognise that Ben, though for what reason she could not guess, was in a towering rage. He might smile and speak lightly but underneath he was quite as angry as she was herself.

Bewildered at the turn the interview had taken, she tried to inject a pacific note.

'Well, I can't deny that. I've never pretended to be original.'

He drew a sharp breath. 'No, you don't pretend much. You fix me with those damned great eyes as if I was some sort of despot about to have you slaughtered. I've never felt so much of an oppressor in my life. Yet I don't—I *can't*—believe that you're really afraid of me. And yet, you've got this transparent honesty and I don't believe that you're pretending when you look at me like that. So what's the reason, Sara? What's the answer to the riddle?'

Sara did not answer him directly. She was not only furious, she was bitterly hurt at his words.

'That's all I am to you,' she managed at last in a choked voice, 'a detective puzzle you're determined to solve. And you don't give a damn how much I might get hurt in the process.'

Ben's eyes had narrowed to slits. 'And how might you get hurt, Sara?'

But she did not fall into the trap laid by the softly, almost idly spoken words; she ignored his interjection.

'Nor have I ever been afraid of you. I am not afraid of anyone.'

That last boast, at least, she thought, was true. One thing her accident had done was to put every other petty anxiety into perspective. She was not afraid of another human being and never would be. She was, though of course she was not going to admit it to Ben, terrified of the way he had made her feel.

And she was even more afraid of what she sensed he could make her feel if he put his mind to it. He could take her over entirely, enter into possession of her very soul so that she would never be whole and independent again.

'If you're not afraid of me, what are you doing

cowering over there behind the desk?' drawled her adversary.

Sara glared at him and walked, with deliberation, round the desk and close up to the chaise longue. He leaned back, laughing face tilted to meet her outraged expression, one long-fingered hand lying lightly along the back of the seat.

'Sit.' It was not a command. It was a challenge.

Sara's eyes flared. But she controlled her tongue with an effort and sat, very precisely, on the far end of the velvet couch. She extended her right hand to him, palm upwards.

'See,' she said sweetly, 'not a tremor.'

'Congratulations.' He stretched his arms high above his head and she tensed uncontrollably waiting for his next movement. The remarkable eyes glinted.

'You see? I only have to flex a muscle and you're on the defensive. What do you think I would do to you, for God's sake? Rend you limb from limb?'

No, worse than that, thought Sara, biting her lip and not answering. He reached out and took her chin, turning her averted face gently towards him. She met his eyes with reluctance, an expression half-fearful, half-ashamed in her own. Ben looked momentarily astounded, and then his eyes were veiled and he was laughing.

'I see. What a dramatic little creature you are.' He leaned back, very much at his ease and his hands began to stroke rhythmically at her throat. Sara swallowed. 'For a girl of your experience, you give a spirited rendition of a shrinking virgin,' he mused. 'Are you frightened of all men, little one, or just me?'

But that was too much for Sara. She might want to avoid hostilities. She did, desperately, want to diffuse the charged atmosphere. But she had her self-respect, and no mocking sophisticate was going to deprive her of it.

'I told you,' she said with commendable lightness, 'I'm not afraid of anyone.' She let a faint note of social regret invade her voice, 'Not even you. I'm sorry.'

It infuriated him, as it was meant to. The stroking hand paused an instant. His hard jaw clenched, she saw with alarm. Then, to her inexpressible relief, he dropped his hand and drew back.

'I'm glad to hear that,' Ben said politely. He looked very cold and distant. 'It relieves my mind of a great weight,' He looked behind him out of the window and then at his watch. 'If you'll forgive me now, I must go and put the storm lantern in the tower.'

Sara was bewildered. 'Storm lantern?'

He gave her a smile which did not reach his eyes. 'Yes, we always put up a light for shipping when there is fog as there is tonight. Or didn't you notice?'

She shook her head.

'It is not unusual, though it does not normally come down so heavy at this time of year. It was very thick when I took Daniella back to the boat. She was half inclined to stay the night, but I—er—dissuaded her.'

Sara was not sure why, but the expression in the smooth voice and the light, disparaging flick of his glance had her blushing fiercely again. She jumped up.

'Then I won't keep you. I'll say goodnight.'

The look he gave her was enigmatic.

'Will you?'

There was a sound outside the window, across the water. Sara jumped.

'Fog horns,' said Ben without emotion. 'I must go and get that light lit. Go to bed, Sara.'

She escaped with more speed than dignity, and flew up the grand curve of the staircase as if the devil were after her. She did not look back, but she was certain that he followed her out of the study and stood in the marble hall looking after her.

CHAPTER EIGHT

In her room, Sara prowled restlessly. Guilio had fastened the shutters earlier, but now she loosed the hasps and swung them back. As Ben had said, the night was shrouded in thick fog. Normally, she could see the lights of Venice, even when there were clouds hiding the stars, but this evening there was nothing. Even the fluted columns of her balcony balustrade looked wafting and insubstantial in the mist.

She slipped open the bolts on the window and went out on to her balcony. She could still hear the sea, hushing and lulling below, but she could not make out the rocks or the distant shape of the boathouse and jetty. There was a faint, bitter breeze but when it fell the air was warm enough. From the lagoon, there came the sounds of horns and bells, presumably used as fog warning, but they were muted in the shrouding mist. For the first time since she had been here, she could not hear the sound of birds. She shivered, and went inside.

The lofty room was cool. No doubt in the winter there would be a log fire blazing in the marble hearth, but now the grate was empty except for a huge copper pot of leaves and flowers. And one could not, thought Sara wryly, warm one's hands at a chrysanthemum, no matter how burning its colours. She retrieved her one warm nightdress from the sandalwood scented drawers in the fifteenth-century armoire, and went to shower.

The bathroom, small and well-lit, was oddly cosy. Sara felt herself relax in its comfort. The difficulties of the day and that last unnerving interview with Ben, faded as she revelled in the warm water. Really, she was being very silly letting him get under her skin like that.

He was only her employer after all. She could leave at any time; especially now that she had enough money for the treatment Dermott Andrews recommended. There was nothing Ben could do to her and she was being ridiculous in allowing him to panic her like that.

She pulled the warm nightdress over her head. It was fine cream wool, with a lace-edged collar and lace cuffs that buttoned with tiny pearl buttons. It had been one of her few extravagancies when she was a working dancer.

Clipping off the light, she went back into her room. And stopped dead.

The lights which she had left burning had been doused and there was now only the soft glow of the bedside reading lamp to illuminate the room. A man's black jacket was lying on one gold damask chair as if it had been stripped off and thrown there carelessly as its owner entered the room. On the chest, blatant intruders among Sara's modest brush and comb and hair grips, lay a pair of silver cuff links, embossed with the Cavalli coat of arms. An untied bow tie had been draped over the mirror.

Sara's eyes went round the room slowly, taking in with a little jolt of shock, each indication that her sanctum had been invaded. She noted every individual object. It was astonishing how, with so small an effort, he had managed to infiltrate his presence into what had previously been her own private place. In horrified fascination, her glance went from one to the other until, with a sense of impending disaster, she came to the intruder himself.

He was reclining on the bed, watching her with undisguised amusement, as he unbuttoned his shirt. Sara flinched. His air of assurance sent a thrill of dismay through her. He looked as if he had every right to be there; as if he expected to be expected. She began to turn over in her mind what she might have said to give him that impression and could recall nothing. A little frantically, she went over every word that had been spoken downstairs in the library.

At last, she said in a voice she did not recognise, 'What are you doing here?'

His smile grew. He undid the last button and slid his arms out of his shirt. The linen fell and he caught it one-handed and tossed it at the chair which housed his jacket. That was all the answer he made.

Sara took a step forward. 'I asked you a question.'

'Darling, I'm always asking you questions, and you never answer any of them,' he retorted looking mischievous. 'I thought it was time I stopped trying to parley and took action.'

She paled. 'I don't know what you mean.'

'Then you're a good deal more stupid than I take you for,' Ben told her drily. He reached out a hand. 'Come here.'

As if mesmerised, she went towards him, her bare feet making no sound on the floor as she moved. He reached out and took her hand, tugging it gently until she gave way and sat abruptly on the bed beside him. Her heart beat painfully fast.

'You and I have done nothing but fence with each other for months,' he said quite gently. 'It's time we stopped.'

His fingers were touching the inside of her wrist, caressing very lightly and delicately. She drew a shivery breath.

'Please,' she said in a low voice, 'don't do that.'

He looked down at what his fingers were doing, unbuttoning the cuff and running a seductive shimmer of sensation along the blue vein thus revealed.

'Why not?'

She was shaking as if she had a fever. She could not answer him. Her throat was dry and her every muscle seemed suspended under the wicked touch that left her feeling paralysed with pleasure.

'Why not, Sara?' the soft voice insisted.

She shook her head helplessly. She could not speak. After a moment, he stopped that insidious stroking and, taking her unresisting hand, lifted it to his lips. As she felt his mouth on the vulnerable skin of her wrist where the pulse was beating fast, Sara gasped.

Her whole body responded. In the charged silence, she felt her heart contract with need. She said his name once, on a sighing breath, barely audible, and then she was turning to him as he reached for her.

It was if time had stopped. Slowly, slowly, she felt her head fall back, her eyes close. He kissed her shoulders, her throat, her quivering eyelids. Those clever hands rid her of her nightdress with practised ease. Even in her daze, she recognised the expertise and was chilled by it. And then she could not think at all.

Ben was stroking every curve, following every contour with his fingertips, watching her body absorbedly. Sara had no thought of denying him, though there was no hint of force in his touch. She felt as if her blood had turned to liquid gold and her whole body was incandescent with what he was doing to her. Her breasts tautened and she yearned towards him, but still he held off from her, teasing her with that tantalising gentleness, and watching, watching. . . .

Her throat arched. She murmured something. She did not know what, then or later, but no matter what the words, they both knew what it was that she wanted. He raised his dark head and gave her a look of total comprehension, of total ownership. And then, her body went out of her control, arching up towards him, offering itself unmistakably for his pleasure. Sara felt his lips travel over every sensitive place that his fingers had discovered. She burned for him. When he kissed one taut breast with agonising gentleness, she clasped him to her fiercely.

Ben was murmuring in his own language, soft words

which she could not detect, that were muffled against the silk of her skin. His hands firmed, lifted her, moved her among the pillows. A faint, distant worry occurred to her. She held him a little away, her palms flat against his chest.

'Ben—I,' she moistened her lips, overcome by shyness. 'You mustn't. . . .'

'Mustn't?' He sent one amused look down the aroused length of her body.

Sara grew agitated. 'No, you don't understand. Please listen to me.'

But he would not. He wanted her. She was not so innocent that she could pretend not to know that. And he was experienced enough to recognise Sara's own need. He was quite gentle, laughing a little, but Sara recognised implacability in the uncompromising strength with which she was held. He would not stop now.

Nor, if she was honest, did she want him to stop. Her every nerve and sinew cried out for him. But he thought her experienced, practised in these arts, as he undoubtedly was himself, and she was suddenly terribly afraid of being betrayed by her ignorance into giving offence.

She said desperately, 'Ben, *please*. . . .'

His eyes had darkened almost to black, she discovered. And there was almost unbearable tension in the set of his mouth. But when he spoke, it was still lightly.

'What's the matter, darling? Did your mother tell you that men like the thrill of the chase? She was right, of course, but the great secret is to know when the chase is over. And yours is.' His voice thickened suddenly. 'I've caught you now, so you might just as well—er—give in gracefully.'

There followed a few moments which Sara was never afterwards to forget. She tried to wriggle away from him but he would not let her go. Or rather, he seemed not to notice that she was attempting to escape. And every move she made aroused them both until she was weeping with helpless longing and he was beyond hearing anything she might say. Sara was boneless as he tumbled her back among the pillows and drove blindly for his own satisfaction.

She was conscious of nothing but pain. She did not think she cried out but her instant rigidity must have told him everything. He stopped as if he had been struck. Then, wordlessly, he wrenched himself away from her and off the bed.

Sara lay still. She felt torn, wrenched apart, light-headed with pain. Nobody had ever told her it could hurt like this. She did not quite believe it.

And then, slowly, the outside world began to return to its place and the pain diminished. She heard the distant fog horns, the faint rumble of the Palazzo's generator, the pad of the man's feet on the floor. She lifted her head, finding that the movement made her feel swimmy and slightly sick. She sank back on to the pillows.

Ben came to her side at once.

'Why didn't you tell me?' His voice was unrecognisable. She opened her eyes. He was standing behind the light, a shadow only, but she could see that he had dressed. She moved her head, trying to bring his expression into focus.

'I tried.' It was a dry little whisper.

There was an unnerving pause while he looked down at her. Sara thought that all her worst fears were realised. She had been betrayed by her inexperience. He would hate her. He would feel that she had tricked him into—well, what? To him it must feel like near-rape. He was not a violent man. He would hate the thought of it. He would surely never forgive her.

Tears began to seep under her closed eyelids. She turned her head away in case he observed them.

'I'm sorry,' she added miserably.

'You're *sorry*!' It ripped out at her as if, just for that moment, he could not contain his fury. Then he reverted to that unfamiliar clipped voice. 'Are you hurt? Can you—move?'

Sara managed a travesty of a smile. 'I'm all right. I'd like to be alone, though.'

'Is that wise? If you can't bear me to stay, I can understand that, but should you be alone? I'll call Vittoria.'

'No!' she cried.

'Or a doctor . . .?'

'Ben,' she said, almost in tears, 'I'm not injured. I don't need anyone. I just need to be alone.'

He said in a low voice, 'I never meant to hurt you so. It never occurred to me——'

But she could not bear to talk of it.

'Go,' she said feverishly. 'Please, just go.'

Again, he paused. She would not look at him. With a gesture that was almost tender, he drew the coverlet from the bottom of the bed up over her shaking body. Then he brushed the hair very gently from her face. Sara sank her teeth down hard into her bottom lip to stop herself crying out to him to take her in his arms and stay.

'Do you want anything?' Ben asked, in that still emotionless voice.

'No.' He still stood there, looking down at her. She managed to add, 'Thank you.'

He said her name under his breath, urgently, but she barely heard him. The threatened storm of weeping was very near, and she did not think she could bear the ultimate humiliation of having him watch that.

'Please,' she said, with a fervour he could not misinterpet, '*please* leave me.'

He turned and went out. The door had barely shut behind him before Sara twisted round and buried her face in the pillow, weeping wildly.

She did not know how she could face him the next morning. She slept fitfully and was awake before six. It was a brilliant day, all sign of last night's fog gone. She paced her balcony in the September sunshine, rehearsing her speech of resignation. She did not know what she was going to say to Uncle Luigi. With his book so very nearly finished, he would see it as a kind of betrayal for her to go now. But Sara was quite clear that she could not bear another encounter like last night's. Nor, she acknowledged to herself, could she bear to be close to Ben, to see him every day, and know that he was denied to her.

When she came downstairs to the breakfast room, she was heavy-eyed. The post that Daniella had brought with her on the previous evening still lay on the console table in the hall. A number of packages, as well as envelopes, for Ben made her wince. It was stupid, she chided herself, to feel as if she had touched molten steel just to see his name printed on a label.

It was not so early that Guilio had not laid the table, though he was surprised to see her. He gave her coffee and promised her rolls which Vittoria had only just put into the oven to bake. In the meantime, would the signorina like orange juice? Fresh pineapple?

Sara declined, but poured herself a huge cup of coffee, added a dash of milk, and took it out on to the terrace. The paved area was a sun trap, as the tubbed geraniums bore witness, and she relaxed on the slatted wooden seat, turning her face up to the sky. It was very peaceful. Some measure of equilibrium returned to her.

When Guilio brought out the hot rolls twenty minutes later she was able to thank him with composure. He grinned at her.

'It is nothing, signorina. This morning, we will

prepare the enormous breakfast, the American breakfast.'

Sara was intrigued. Uncle Luigi assured her that the consumption of protein at breakfast time was a sign of an uncultivated and brutal civilisation, and Ben, she knew, always breakfasted in his own rooms. Was Ben going to break his rule and join them? She swallowed, her peace gone. While she debated whether she had the courage to ask—or the courage instead to wait and see—Guilio explained.

'The Principessa will be here almost immediately. There was a telephone call last night, very late.'

'Oh,' said Sara, not knowing if she was disappointed or relieved.

'She was held up by the fog. She stayed in the city last night, with friends, but she said she would be with us for breakfast.'

'Does Signor Luigi know?'

'Simonetta told him when she took up his morning chocolate. He will no doubt be up soon.'

And so, indeed, it proved. The Principessa, arriving in style in a craft that looked more like a racing speedboat than any sort of ferry, came racing up the stony path into the arms of her brother-in-law, a little after nine o'clock.

'Honey, you're looking so well,' she congratulated him, 'And Guilio—no problems with running the world, eh?'

She went straight into the kitchen. There were hugs all round, a great clattering announced the commencement of the American breakfast, and the Principessa, nibbling at one of Vittoria's doughnuts, allowed herself to be led out on to the terrace and introduced to Sara. In all this activity, there was no sign of her son and no comment from the Principessa on his absence.

Sara, shaking a slightly sugary hand, found that the Principessa was not only a good deal younger than she had expected, but that she was responsible for Ben's devastating blue eyes. In the Principessa's case, they were expertly lilac shadowed and fringed with slightly less expert sooty lashes that had left smudges underneath. It did not detract from her gamine charm. She looked like a warm, tolerant, energetic schoolgirl, in spite of the lines on her face.

She laughed, shaking back the hair which was confined with a Gucci scarf scrunched into a hairband, and gave Sara a wide smile.

'So you're the dragon that has been keeping Luigi at his studies,' she remarked. 'I don't think I'm as sorry for him as I was. How do you like Venice, my dear?'

'Mediaeval or present-day?' asked Sara with amusement. It was an effort to talk to anyone at the moment, but she found Ben's mother easier than she would have believed possible.

The Principessa gave a gurgle of laughter. 'I see what it is. Luigi has kept you tied to his infernal maps and you haven't seen a thing of the city.'

'Marianne, you wrong me,' Uncle Luigi protested. 'Sara has been wandering whenever she wanted.'

'I usually hitch a ride with Salvatore,' Sara added in corroboration.

'And I took her round myself the first day. Not that Ben thought that was sufficient,' he added in a voice full of meaning, which Sara could not interpret, 'because he took her round himself afterwards. Took her everywhere. Even shopping.'

His sister-in-law gave him a quick look.

'Ben is still here then, I did wonder. . . .'

'He has been here all summer.' said Uncle Luigi darkly. Again there was that private meaning which was lost on Sara. Perhaps he was telling the Principessa that Ben could not keep away from Daniella Vecellio, she thought miserably.

She turned to look out over the bay, but not before

she had seen the visitor's eyebrows fly up. Then the Principessa collected herself, a quick look in Sara's direction saying to Sara more eloquently than words that family affairs could not be discussed in front of a stranger.

Uncle Luigi gave a faint nod, obviously agreeing with that silent message.

'I'll press on with that index,' Sara told him, trying to sound normal.

The Principessa gave her a charming smile. 'My dear child, don't let me drive you back to the maps. Stay and tell me how you like Venice; how you like the Palazzo now that Ben is letting me put it to rights at last?'

Sara found she could not meet those friendly eyes. If the Principessa knew—if she had seen her in Ben's arms last night and his cold face afterwards—would she still be so charming, so friendly?

'N-no. I must work. I'm behind. . . .'

And Sara fled, without waiting for a response, desperate to carry her burden of shame and guilt off into the comparative privacy of the library. She was unaware that the other two looked after her in consternation.

She sank on to a straight-backed chair behind the large mahogany desk and straightened Uncle Luigi's working notes with feverish desperation. She would have to go. She could not stay and face Ben. She would have to leave the work on Uncle Luigi's thesis in a reasonable order so that somebody else could take over. She would have to make up some story to tell him. Perhaps he could be induced to be her go-between to Ben. He knew something, suspected something, she was sure. She had seen him looking at her with compassion. If she could tell him a little——

But her mind closed it off. She shut her eyes in a sudden excess of anguish. No, she could not tell Uncle Luigi, or indeed anyone else, anything. She would never forget the way Ben had looked last night. He had sounded so cold, so remote, as if she had suddenly become a creature from another planet.

As I suppose I have, she thought, shivering a little. This morning she had felt so cold when she awoke, in spite of the sun blazing in through the shutters he had left unfastened last night. She had slept fitfully and when she woke she had reached for him. It was as if her body expected him to be here. Her body, so long an accomplished servant, had overnight turned into a cruel and demanding tyrant. She had woken with an almost palpable need for him and had hardly believed that he was not there.

Sara pressed the backs of her hands against her dry eyes. She was aware of a rising panic. She felt disorientated, shaken, an alien to herself. And her only fellow creature in the new world in which she found herself was the grim-faced man who had left her last night. Who did not want or need her. Who would indeed be appalled if he knew the extent of her own want and needs.

She wondered whether he would tell Daniella and flinched as if at the touch of a whip. She could imagine it: two sophisticates conversing on the pillow after their own infinitely accomplished night of passion. Daniella would be reproachful, faintly annoyed perhaps. And Ben. Well, he was not an unkind man and he would probably be sorry for what had happened. His imagined pity cut Sara like a knife. She dropped her head in her hands.

And was interrupted. Guilio, smiling gravely, asked whether she could spare the signore a few moments in his study.

Sara went cold. 'Now?' she asked, hoping for a reprieve.

Guilio gave her his normal benevolent smile. Here at least was someone who could not tell from her face how fathoms out of her depth she had swum last night; what a pitiable creature she had become.

'He asked for you as soon as I found you, signorina,' Guilio told her, faintly puzzled by the open desperation in the candid green eyes. 'I think he is busy. There was a lot for him to deal with in the post that Signora Vecellio brought, I believe. He did not,' added Guilio, anxious to take the shadow from her eyes, 'sound angry, if you understand me.'

No, he would not be angry. Regretful, sorry for her. Not angry.

She swallowed. 'If he is busy, perhaps it won't take long.'

She squared her shoulders and went with a courage that leaked away with every stair she climbed up the staircase and along the little intercommunicating passage.

This time, she did not have to knock. The door was open.

Sara slipped in quietly and stopped dead. The reason for all those empty picture frames became clear. For they were no longer empty. They were full of shadowy shapes and each one was illuminated. And Ben, his broad shoulders hunched in concentration, was sitting in a swivel chair in front of them.

'X-rays,' she gasped, forgetting her distress in simple astonishment.

Ben whipped round, as if he had been shot. She took a step backwards, flushing.

'I'm sorry. I didn't mean to startle you. I thought you wanted to see me. The door was open,' she explained, confused.

For a moment, he did not speak. The firm jaw was set uncompromisingly and his eyes were almost black.

He said curtly, 'There's no need to apologise. I asked to see you.'

It was, Sara thought in bewilderment, almost

inconceivable that he had ever held her in his arms, let alone made passionate love to her. She had never felt such a distance between them. She thought that this morning he must have recalled that she was his employee and decided to treat her accordingly.

She lifted her chin and said coolly. 'What about?'

His mouth compressed. 'Don't play games, Sara. You know perfectly well what about.'

'If,' she said with a calm distaste of which she was inordinately proud, 'it is about what happened last night, I would prefer not to discuss it.'

Ben's eyes flashed, but he leaned back in his chair and put his fingertips together while he contemplated her as if, she thought furiously, she were an applicant for a job.

'I see,' he said at last politely. Too politely. 'And what if *I* want to talk about it? There were two of us involved, you will recall.'

'I do indeed. And neither of us, as I remember, showed up particularly well.' Sara regarded him levelly. 'There is not an apology that would cover it. And recriminations aren't my style.'

He gave her an unreadable look.

'No,' he said at last, startling her, 'I don't suppose they are. So what do you suggest we do? Acknowledge each other civilly when we meet on the stairs and pretend it never happened?' The mockery in the smooth voice was almost savage.

Sara flinched but replied evenly, 'No, I don't think either of us could manage civility, do you? I must go, of course.'

'No!' It blasted out of him like an explosion, and she took an involuntary step backwards as he surged out of his chair towards her. 'I knew you'd say that. I knew you'd try to run away. You've been running ever since you set eyes on me, God knows why.'

'Last night should have told you why,' she said in a frozen voice.

He lost all colour. 'You don't mean that.'

She turned her head so that the fall of hair hid her expression. She was trembling convulsively.

Ben said urgently, 'Sara, last night, I know I lost my head. I wasn't thinking clearly, and I—frightened you. Hurt you. But you must believe I would never have done it deliberately.'

'I'm sure you never meant to hurt me,' Sara conceded. She turned her shoulder on him. 'But I'm afraid that doesn't make any difference to the way I feel.'

He took an impetuous step towards her. She had the feeling that he was clamping down hard on whatever emotions were riding him. Anger, she thought, was uppermost. But when he spoke, his tone was calm, reasonable.

'Sara, I know what I did last night was unforgivable. I shall never cease to regret it.'

Her hands clenched, though she said nothing. It was just as she thought: he could not bear to think about it. He would want her, and everything that reminded him of his loss of control, out of his sight.

'But I didn't plan it that way. You must believe that. It just happened. A sort of horrible accident, if you like. It was a spur of the moment thing.'

Sara thought she would shrivel up with the pain. She folded her hands tightly together and pressed them against her ribcage as if she were applying pressure to a real physical hurt. So he had never really wanted her. She had been there and he had been in an uncertain mood. On the spur of the moment—how that phrase more than anything else, revealed how little he had cared, then or now.

Still not looking at him, she said, 'I'm not bearing any grudges, Ben. I told you, I don't think either of us comes out of last night too well. It was at least partly my fault.'

In exasperation he interrupted, 'It's not a question of *fault*. Or blame.' His voice gentled. 'Look, Sara. Something happened last night that neither you nor I can turn our backs on. No matter how much you may want to.'

She was shaking her head. 'Don't you understand? It's over. Finished. It was an accident, as you said. All right, the accident happened, but now it's in the past.' She rounded on him, eyes wild, hair flying. 'I'll go. At once, if you like. Today. I'll do anything. Only I—do—not—want—to—talk—about—it.'

He said something profane under his breath. Reaching out, he took her by the elbows.

'Don't, Sara. Ah, don't tear yourself apart like this. . . .'

They were interrupted by a strident peal from the telephone on his desk. For a moment, he hesitated, casting a slightly harassed look at the machine, returning to inspect anxiously Sara's distraught face. Then the machine screamed again and his hands fell away and he went to it.

'Cavalli,' he said curtly. There was silence. Then he said, 'No, I haven't looked at it. The X-rays looked reasonably hopeful. I sent them off to you. What?' There was a pause while he listened intently. Then he said with exaggerated patience, 'I told you, I haven't looked at it. It only arrived last night and I haven't even opened it yet. I'll do it today and call you back. I can't talk now, Mario, I'm busy.'

He put the telephone down with the sketchiest of goodbyes.

The conversation had given Sara a respite. She had pulled herself together, pushed the hair out of her eyes, and was once more reasonably in command of herself. Sufficiently in command of herself, at least, to know that she had to keep out of that seductive hold.

Before he could speak, she said, 'I'll pack at once. I'll

leave a list of what else has to be done on Uncle Luigi's manuscript. It will be easy enough to get someone to type out the index. And there isn't anything else much.'

'You are not,' he said with resolution, 'leaving.'

Sara was at the door. She looked at him over her shoulder. He was incredibly handsome, in spite of the menacing glint in his eyes. She longed to go to him, to smoothe the dishevelled hair and run her fingers down the fierce lines beside his nose and mouth until he smiled again. Just for a moment she hesitated. But then she recalled the pain of loving and knew that she could not bear to give and give and give and receive only his occasional spur of the moment attention in return.

'You can't stop me,' she said sadly.

And left.

CHAPTER NINE

THE clinic was in an old mansion by the lakeside surrounded by trees. The patients stayed in exquisitely appointed rooms in the house. The treatment rooms and the operating theatre were in a new block, hidden behind conifers. The gardens, which sloped graciously down to the edge of the lake, were beautiful. The lawns were carefully tended and the banks of shrubs and trees grew in hothouse profusion.

It took Sara some days to register all these advantages and rather more to appreciate them. She had arrived in a state of numbness bordering on shock and had barely communicated with the staff, except for brief technical discussions on the subject of her ankle for a week.

She still shuddered, remembering her departure from the Palazzo. Uncle Luigi had been hurt and vociferous. The Principessa was puzzled but very kind. And the servants had been so angelically understanding that she still wept to think about it. All except Simonetta, of course.

'So he sent you packing at last,' she said to Sara, by way of farewell. 'I heard the signora telling him to,' she said. A spiteful look came into the smouldering little face and Simonetta quoted what were unmistakably Daniella's words, 'I've had enough of her mooning over you, *amore*. Send her back where she came from.' She even caught Daniella's faintly bored intonation.

Sara was already so stunned, though, that she barely reacted, though she heard the malice in Simonetta's voice and the words came back to haunt her later. At the time, however, they seemed trivial in comparison with the fact that, knowing she was leaving, Ben made no attempt either to stop her or to bid her farewell.

While Salvatore ripped out a violent rebuke, Sara returned the girl's hostile look with gentle dignity.

'Goodbye, Simonetta,' she said quietly, finally.

The girl gave an infuriated squeak and flounced off along the shore, the bright skirts swaying.

At last, painfully, she began to ask Salvatore's advice about a place to stay. Somewhere not too expensive she explained: a good clean pensione, if he knew of one. He did. A good respectable place run by a kind-hearted couple of whom the signore approved.

That made Sara jump and brought the colour to her pale cheeks. She did not, she said in agitation, want to go anywhere that the signore might know of. She wanted to disappear, not to be found by him. Salvatore was to promise not to tell him. Soothingly, impassively, Salvatore promised. And delivered her up safely to the best small family hotel in Venice.

She had telephoned Dermott Andrews at once who, in turn, had contacted the clinic in Como. Yes, they could receive Miss Romana at once; yes, her treatment could begin immediately under the care of one of the residents. The specialist who would have overall charge of her case was unfortunately away at present but his assistant was very experienced.

The assistant proved to be a cheerful German girl called Gunilla. Her ankle, she congratulated Sara, was already a good deal better than the state revealed by the X-rays that Mr Andrews had sent which were now with the professor. Gunilla would have to await his endorsement of her treatment, of course, but she was already of the opinion that another operation could be avoided. She saw no reason why Sara should not soon be dancing again and as well as ever.

Sara should have been overjoyed. She felt that, in failing to weep with relief, she was letting down the medical staff who all obviously expected her to be emotional about their miraculous cure. And she did try. She was truly appreciative, she told Gunilla; it was wonderful news.

The German girl, looking at her with considerable shrewdness, had not been unduly surprised. She was fairly certain that Miss Romana was in very great trouble. Worse trouble than even a damaged ankle, she thought. She wondered whether she had perhaps received some news which meant that her career was finished anyway, even if she did recover full use of the limb. Or perhaps it was something more personal. The notes did not mention anything but then these English notes were never very informative about the psychology of the patient, were they? The English, said Gunilla, discussing her most puzzling patient with her superior, were so cold.

He did not ask to see Sara for three weeks. And Sara, exercising grimly through all the hours of daylight, sitting through painful manipulation of the injured ankle in determined silence, did not even notice. He was the doctor in charge of her case and though she did not see him, she was not even surprised. She never thought about it at all. She was doing her best not to think about anything except her treatment and full recovery and then the resumption of her career.

So she was utterly unprepared when he walked in one day when Sara was in the exercise room with the pshysiotherapist and Gunilla, who accompanied him, announced cheerfully, 'You will be glad to meet Professor Cavalli at last, Miss Romana.'

Sara sat as if she had been turned to stone. The physiotherapist, suddenly getting no co-operation from her most compliant patient, looked up in surprise. The girl looked blind, as if she had been struck. The physiotherapist shrugged, not bothering to look at the doctors. Another woman bowled over by the glamorous

Professor Cavalli, that was obvious. And he, of course, would be as unmoved as he always was. She went back to work, ignoring them.

Sara licked suddenly dry lips. It was a nightmare. It could not be happening. It was very clear that he had already known. There was no shock in the expressionless blue eyes.

He gave her a cool nod. 'I hear your course of treatment is proving satisfactory, Miss Romana. My assistant tells me she does not, after all, recommend surgery.'

Sara was blank.

'That is very good news,' he prompted her gently.

'I—yes,' she agreed at last, aware that Gunilla was looking at her strangely.

He turned away to look at charts, the notes that Gunilla had carefully made, to consult with the physiotherapist. Sara could only stare at the back of his head, so familiar, now so desperately a stranger's. She felt her whole body grow colder and colder. He gave no sign that he was aware of her at all, except as an interesting case. Well, she had always known that he was intrigued by her; he had told her as much. And now he had her pinned down under his microscope for inspection at his leisure. She would never have believed that she could feel so hurt, so betrayed.

The physiotherapist spoke, first gently, then quite sharply, to recall her attention. Sara stared at her uncomprehending for a second. Then, realising that she was requested to perform the prescribed sequence of exercises for the Professor's benefit, Sara went mechanically through the routine of foot and leg movements.

He watched her coolly, without discernible expression. At no time did his eyes meet hers. He hunkered down at her foot, explored it with those long, sensitive fingers, that she would have known the touch of anywhere, without seeing them. She flinched violently from the contact, to the surprise of the two women who were used to her bearing pain without protest. His face darkened, but he did not look up. He completed his examination, manipulating the ankle, and at last stood up, expressing himself satisfied. Throughout, he addressed her as Miss Romana.

And then, nodding pleasantly, he was gone.

Sara found she was shaking so badly that she could not begin to get her foot to obey her. In the end, even the physiotherapist admitted defeat, and, for the first time in the treatment, dismissed her before her full hour was completed. She limped heavily out and back to the sanctuary of her room, a small chalet by the lake. She sat there, staring as if mesmerised at the telephone.

Ben never rang. She saw him seldom, never alone, and when they met he was always impersonally polite. She thought her heart would break.

When Gunilla told her that her treatment would be complete in three days, she received it numbly. She was hardly more excited by the letter she had from Sir Gerald promising her solo roles in the forthcoming season and insisting she return to start rehearsing at once.

Nor, when Robert Ericsson made a dramatic appearance by her side when she was walking one day by the edge of the lake, did he get the reception he felt was his due.

'Have you hurt yourself, too?' she asked politely, after greeting him. 'Is that why you are here?'

'No,' he said in a voice that throbbed. 'I've come for you. I want you back.'

Sara was incredulous. After the months of silence, the callous desertion, he thought he could walk back into her life and be welcomed. Robert, spoiled, successful, famous Robert had decided what he wanted. She thought it rather sad. Though it was not without its amusing side too.

She said gently, 'I didn't know. You never wrote.'

'Well—I wasn't sure—I mean, you might still have been ill.'

He was floundering. Sara realised in dawning amazement that he had returned to her side when, and only when, he had heard she had recovered. She should have been angry, but he was so transparent that she found it hard not to laugh.

'How did you know that I was better?' she asked unsteadily.

'Er—Sir Gerald dropped me a hint actually,' he confessed. His handsome features faintly tinged with pink.

Sara turned her head away to hide her expression. So, Sir Gerald was making mischief, no doubt feeling that Robert Ericsson deserved payment in his own coin. Presumably, Sir Gerald had, in his inimitably suave style, implied that Robert, in abandoning Sara at the crisis in her life, had passed up a good thing. She could imagine the scene vividly. Sir Gerald would, no doubt, be very pleased with himself at having exacted vengeance.

'I see. I shall be working for him again, of course,' Sara said neutrally.

'Then we must get engaged again. I *have* to see you. You're the only woman I've ever loved,' he told her in accents which clearly said that she ought to consider herself highly honoured.

'Thank you,' she said drily, 'but our engagement ended, as I recall, some time ago. And I don't believe in resurrecting such things.'

For a moment, she thought he would stamp his foot. He looked like a thwarted child.

'You're being vindictive,' he said. 'You're bearing grudges. I had to think of my career. I had to go to the States and you obviously had to stay where the doctors were. And it was *you* who broke it off. If you only look at it from my point of view. . . .'

But Sara interrupted him.

'No,' she said quietly. 'Look at it from mine, for once. I loved you. I thought I could rely on you. I was badly hurt—not just physically—and you let me down. I don't want to go through that again.'

He stared at her in silence, obviously puzzled, slightly offended. 'Again? But you're all right now, aren't you? Sir Gerald said you were fully recovered.'

The suspicion, the horrified retreat as he contemplated the possibility were too much for Sara's composure. She laughed aloud. Robert looked even more alarmed.

'No, no,' she said at last, when she could speak. 'I'm well. They tell me I'm guaranteed in full running order.'

He frowned blackly. 'Then why say otherwise? Why lie?'

'I didn't,' Sara said patiently. 'I said I didn't want to risk it again, and I don't. Why, good heavens, Robert, anything could happen: I could be ill again. I could be disliked by the critics, or the public, or both. And one day, I shall have to stop dancing. That's ignoring all the usual domestic disasters that beset a marriage. No, no.' She leaned across and patted his cheek in sudden compunction, 'I would know that I could never rely on you. And you, if you are honest, don't want to be relied on.'

He bit his lip.

'You're punishing me,' he said at last in an accusing voice.

Sara sighed. 'Oh do stop thinking about yourself for once, Robert. Of course I'm not punishing you. I'm looking after myself.'

'But what will people *say*?' he burst out.

Thoroughly bewildered, Sara shook her head.

'Say?'

'About us. Me. When you make your comeback and I'm not there. They all knew we were engaged.'

Still puzzled, Sara said, 'So?'

'So they'll think I abandoned you when you broke your ankle. If I'm not around,' said Robert, clearly contemplating an unfavourable press in the gossip columns and worried about it. He turned glittering eyes on her. 'People are so fickle. And audiences for modern music are thin enough anyway. I can't afford bad publicity.'

She said soothingly, 'We can still be friends. You can come to my first night. All the gossips can say is that we were very young when we got engaged and now we are older.'

He thought about that, his frown lightening somewhat.

'Will it do, do you think?'

'It will have to,' she said solemnly, 'because I'm not marrying you to improve your public image.'

He did flush at that, looking ashamed for the first time in their interview.

Sara relented.

'Come on. We'll go back to my chalet and I'll give you some coffee and you can tell me all about what you've been doing,' she said consolingly.

If Sara had been really worried about the possibility of breaking Robert's heart, she would have been reassured by the ease with which he was deflected into talking about himself. He spent pretty well the whole day with her and never once, in all the hours, asked her what she had been doing or how she had supported herself in the intervening months.

Which was just as well because she would not have known how to answer him. It would have been impossible to tell Robert about Ben. She did not know how she would even have begun to try. But it was equally impossible to talk about her life without mentioning Ben.

Ben Cavalli, realised Sara at last, had infiltrated every

corner of her life. He had become the measure by which she judged. Beside him Robert seemed a lightweight—selfish, shallow and, for all his glamour, something of a fool. She knew that, before she met Ben, she would never have laughed at Robert. Never have had the perception to see how funny Robert's childishness really was.

And where did that leave her now? Ben filled her thoughts. Her every encounter brought her mind back to him. She never fell asleep without dreaming of him. She never woke up without looking, instinctively, for his presence beside her. She wanted to talk to him, to share all she felt with him. She needed his support in the coming ordeal of returning to dancing. She longed for his touch.

I'm in love with him, she thought. It turned her cold. He did not want her. He had made it plain. That last, devastating night in the Palazzo had been an accident. A spur of the moment thing, as he had said, and she would never now be able to forget what he had said.

Perhaps I'll get over it, she told herself, without much conviction. I got over Robert. But she had not been much more than a child when she fell in love with Robert. When she met Ben, she was a woman, tempered already by cruel experience. This one would not be easily shaken off. This love, she said the word to herself deliberately, was probably for ever.

So when Gunilla told her that Professor Cavalli would like to see her before she left the clinic, Sara refused. Panic-stricken, barely holding on to her poise, with absolute conviction she said that she could not see Professor Cavalli.

Gunilla was surprised. 'But he asked most particularly,' she pointed out.

'I thought all my medical examinations were over,' protested Sara.

'Oh, they are. You are signed off. Discharged—is

that the word? But Professor Cavalli has been most impressed by your courage and determination,' said kindly Gunilla. 'I think he would like to say a personal goodbye. To wish you good luck, you know.'

'I know,' said Sara in a hollow voice. She pulled herself together. 'Look, I'm sorry to sound ungracious, but I've got to go at once.' She sought desperately for a reason to account for this acceleration and found a good one. 'My fiancé has arrived to take me home,' Robert owed her that, at least, she thought, 'and has to leave now. In fact, I'm already late. I must go. Thank you for everything. Goodbye.'

And she bundled out of the chalet and into the waiting taxi without a backward look. If she had cast one at Gunilla, she would have seen that the young doctor was looking very thoughtful as she closed up the chalet and went back to the main block to tell Professor Cavalli that his star patient had fled.

Because that was what it was, Gunilla thought. A barely disguised panic-stricken flight.

Sara, huddled miserably in her taxi, could not dismiss thoughts of Ben. She wondered what he would have said to her if she had gone to him. What he would have done. Surely, he could not just have shaken her hand and wished her well, as Gunilla had suggested? But when had he shown any signs of wanting to do anything else?

And he would marry soon, if the servants had been right. Marry Daniella, or someone like her, someone elegant and poised, a graceful hostess for his, no doubt, full social life. She had seen nothing of that side of his life at all. She had known him only in his most private aspect, as a scruffy beachcomber, an affectionate nephew, a reclusive worker. And a lover, an unwelcome voice reminded her.

She flinched and began feverishly to read the details on her flight ticket. With determination, she did not think about Ben Cavalli again. If he crept unbidden into her thoughts, she took herself to task and instantly concentrated fiercely on something else. She might be in love with him but she was *not*, she said to herself, going to let it ruin everything else in her life.

She never mentioned his name to anybody, and, in the ensuing months of gruelling work, nobody ever mentioned his name to her. She did sometimes, though she tried to suppress it, wonder whether he was yet married, but she heard nothing.

And that, she told herself firmly, was all for the best.

CHAPTER TEN

SARA sat in her dressing room and looked round with pleasure. It was still relatively tidy, but she knew that, by the end of the evening's performance, there would be costumes and headdresses and ballet shoes strewn everywhere. The garishly lit dressing table, now neatly set with hairpins and make-up combs and an enormous pot of cotton-wool swabs, would be covered in the debris left by quick changes of character. Sara smiled with pleasure.

Her dresser looked up from the rainbow-coloured chiffon she was pressing.

'Worried, Miss Romana?'

Sara gave a little shiver. It was madness to admit to stage fright, bad luck to deny it. So she evaded the question.

'It's the first time I've danced in London for two years.'

The dresser was a new girl. Sir Gerald had hired her because she was deft and kind and lived close enough to the theatre not to have an excuse for being late. But she did not know a lot about dancing or the company she was working for.

'I'd heard you'd hurt your foot. Is it better now?'

Sara stretched the ankle in question, now becomingly encased in palest green, and rotated it experimentally. Not a twinge. It felt as she was now sure it was, tough as whipcord. But, superstitiously, she was not admitting it in the dressing room.

'We'll find out tonight,' was all she said.

The door opened behind her and Sir Gerald, resplendent in chestnut velvet smoking jacket and startling cravat, appeared in the doorway. He was bearing a tight bunch of violets. He knew as well as Sara that she was quite likely to be presented with a number of formal bouquets after the performance. But Sir Gerald knew that violets were what she had bought herself in the smokey evenings after college on the way home to her rented room. And he had always, ever since she first began to dance solo for him, brought her violets before the performance.

The dresser was taken aback. They were less than the magnificent gift she expected an impressario to give his brightest star. It was widely rumoured that the return of Sara Romana had created such attention in the world of dancing that Sir Gerald's company was being invited all over the world on the strength of it.

Sara, unaware that the dresser was shocked by the inadequacy of Sir Gerald's floral tribute, gravely pushed forward the old fishpaste jar in which she always put them. Sir Gerald poured water into it from the carafe on the dressing table, and Sara, removing the elastic band from the frail stems, arranged the little flowers with pleasure.

Sir Gerald inspected her critically. She was wearing her costume for the first ballet in which she was one of the four equal principal dancers. They were distinguished, even in the programme, only by the colour of their costume. Hers was green. Her deep auburn hair, brushed till it shone, was done in an elaborate plait, interwoven with green and yellow ribbons and silk flowers.

'Pretty,' said Sir Gerald decisively. 'It's a mistake to put you in pale colours. That grass green is just right.'

Sara stopped fussing with her flowers. 'It's lovely,' she agreed. 'Ann looked gorgeous in the eau de nil, of course.'

Sir Gerald smiled at the mention of the dancer who had left the company for an engagement in Denmark.

'Yes, but she was blonde. Your colouring demands something more intense. To say nothing of your character,' he added reflectively.

Sara raised her finely marked brows. 'Are you telling me I'm a prima donna?' she teased.

Sir Gerald, however, was serious. 'No, it's not quite that. But you always seem to feel things a little more than my other dancers. Always have, I suppose. But since the accident. . . .' He stopped. 'Anyway, you're deeper than you were. Nothing melodramatic—just more sensitive, more profound. You might,' he added in congratulatory tones, 'be turning into a really *tragic* ballerina.'

'Tragic ballerinas,' said Sara drily, 'have limited uses. I'd rather stay versatile.'

'You always will be that, as long as you keep your sense of humour. You have the lightness,' Sir Gerald told her.

He stood up as the tannoy system began to rumble with instructions to the backstage staff.

'I've got a party,' he said, making a face. As a founding father of the company, he had to do a good deal of official entertaining which, being basically a shy man, he detested. 'I'll come round at the second interval if I can. And I rely on you to come and hold my hand afterwards. It's supper at Rousseau's,' he said in a voice of deepest gloom, naming one of London's most select restaurants.

Sara laughed and assured him of her support.

The evening was a triumph. She was just nervous enough to feel stretched to her peak. In the final ballet, to Robert's music, she danced the part that had been created for her. She knew she had never danced it better. She danced as if there were no words, and she had never had any medium of expression but her pliant body. In the final bars, reaching towards her partner in helpless, hopeless longing, she forgot all about the technical difficulties, the jumps, the backward flips and her bone-wrenching tiredness. She recalled only the despair of a love that could neither be admitted nor returned. As she flung herself into the consuming light of rising sun at the end of the ballet, the audience gave a gasp of pure grief.

It was as Sir Gerald had predicted. She had become a tragic performer. As the curtain closed, there was a hushed pause and then, at the final swish, a tumult of cheering and clapping arose.

In the wings Sara was dazed. Her partner in the last ballet was James Kingdom, an old friend. It was he who urged her out to face the rapturous audience. She clung tightly to his hand, though James tried to disengage himself, to step back and allow her to take the applause on her own. Flowers rained down on them, some individual roses, some whole posies. Laughing, James managed to free himself from Sara's clutch and set about collecting the flowers from the boards and presenting them to her. Soon her slender figure was all but engulfed.

It went on, it seemed to Sara, for hours. She was exhausted, physically and emotionally. Her feet—though she noted not her damaged ankle—were burning, and her every muscle was shaky with the strain that had been imposed on it. But she still took Sir Gerald's hand and curtsied prettily; led the conductor forward; curtsied again to the clamouring crowd. Till at last, exhausted in their turn, they let her go.

Backstage was surprisingly quiet. The last ballet was a duet, and all the dancers except James and herself had changed and gone before she left the stage. Indeed, a good many had gone round to the front to watch the last ballet in performance.

In her dressing room, Sara sank on to her bench, grateful for the blessed silence. When the door opened, she thought it was her dresser, and looked up with a faint smile.

It was, however, another and totally unexpected visitor.

'My dear, you were tremendous,' said the Principessa, calmly closing the door behind her. 'I see why Gerald was so desperate to get you back. I had no idea ballet could be so exciting.'

Sara stared at her blankly. The Principessa gave her a slightly rueful smile.

'I guess you didn't expect to see me. I asked Gerald not to tell you I was here. It took me a long time to get up courage to come and talk. I don't normally interfere, you know. Ben wouldn't like it.'

Sara whitened. 'Does—Professor Cavalli—know you're here?'

His mother looked amused. 'Good God, no. He'd murder me. But I had to talk to you—since it seems that he refuses to.'

Sara felt as if she had received a blow over the heart. She sat still, breathing carefully, then leaned forward and began to remove her make-up with a hand that shook only slightly.

'What happened between you two? It seemed ideal.' There was no mistaking the Principessa's puzzlement. 'What went wrong?'

Sara's hand stilled. How could she answer? She could not say, 'What went wrong was that I fell in love with him. I'd been hurt and I'd built up the walls and he just razed them all to the ground. Robert hurt me, but when I fell in love with Ben I was not a child any longer, I was a grown woman. I didn't want to fall in love, and when it was over, I was empty and broken. I gave him my body, which is everything I know and everything I am, and he told me he only wanted it as a spur of the moment impulse. It went wrong because it mattered to me and not to Ben.' No she could not say that.

'Sara, he's desperately unhappy. He's working too hard, drinking too much.'

'It is,' Sara said with precision, 'none of my business. But if you think that his unhappiness is due to a lady, you should talk to Signora Vecellio, not me.' She stood up. 'Excuse me, I must shower. Dancing,' she added with a flash of irony, 'may look ethereal but it's awfully sweaty work.'

'Yes, I'm sure,' said the Principessa absently. 'Did you *really* believe Ben was having an affair with Daniella? Did he know you thought that? Does he know now?'

'As I say, it's none of my business.'

To Sara's immense relief her dresser arrived. She gathered up the discarded costume and ballet shoes which were the first thing that Sara had removed, and asked whether she should call a cab to take Sara to Rousseau's.

'Oh, don't bother,' said the Principessa, with a charming smile, 'I always have a car when I'm in London. You can come with me, Sara.'

It was not what Sara wanted, but she could hardly refuse. She showered quickly, spraying herself with her favourite perfume which Sir Gerald always said smelled like snowdrops, and dressed in a dark tailored suit. It was extravagantly severe, relieved only by the violets which her dresser had bound into a button hole for her and pinned on the lapel of the jacket.

The Principessa regarded her approvingly.

'Very elegant. You have the style of the prima ballerina, haven't you, Sara?'

Sara smiled. 'I have my own style. When you're very poor and on your own, as I used to be, you can't afford anyone else's.'

'Yes.' The Principessa was thoughtful. 'Luigi told us about that. I must say, to look at you, no one would believe you'd ever been an impoverished orphan.'

'I would,' said Sara quietly. 'When something is part of yourself you don't forget it.'

The older woman gave a lopsided smile that reminded Sara painfully of Ben's. 'I'm glad to hear it, my dear. As I'm sure Ben will be,' she added obscurely. 'And now, shall we go and eat?'

The restaurant was crowded although it was well past eleven when they arrived. Someone, presumably Sir Gerald, must have told the Press where they would be dining, because Sara faced a barrage of cameras and questions the moment she got out of the Principessa's Mercedes. She smiled and posed for the photographers a couple of times, and then, pleading hunger, managed to force her way through the little group. Laughing, they let her go, and she collected yet another posy from a cameraman in the newsreel party, before she gained the warmth and light of the restaurant.

At Sir Gerald's table there were perhaps twenty people. Sara hesitated, dreading whom she might see, but Ben was not among them. So the Principessa had not lied when she said that she was acting independently of her son. Sara was both relieved and bitterly disappointed. It would have been a strange, painful pleasure to have seen him again, and in the car she had braced herself for it. Now she felt oddly let down.

She ate little. She was toasted in champagne, at which she only sipped, and Sir Gerald made a speech to which she lent half an ear. A party atmosphere prevailed, but she and James, her partner in the last ballet of the evening, were both drooping with fatigue. He made to leave, and his wife, a long-standing friend, made gestures at Sara to offer her a lift home. Sara hesitated. She was tired, but she knew that to accept their offer would take them out of their way. She looked hesitantly at Sir Gerald.

The Principessa, intercepting that look, leaned forward.

'You must be exhausted,' she said in her warm voice. 'The rest of us will probably go on for hours. But that's no reason for you to stay. Why don't you take my car and go home?'

'Oh, I couldn't,' Sara protested instinctively.

'Nonsense, my dear. I won't leave for hours, and my driver will have nothing else to do.' She stood up. 'I'll call him.'

The car arrived in ten minutes, just as James and Anne were in the middle of saying their farewells. Sara seized the opportunity to leave with them, receiving a kiss from Sir Gerald and a warm hug from James on the now-deserted pavement. The chauffeur, standing with the door open to the seat beside him, was impassive as the people who had followed them out into the street embraced and congratulated Sara and James with slightly drunken enthusiasm.

At last, they let her go, and Sara slid into the warmth of the Mercedes with an audible sigh of relief. The chauffeur closed the door on her, adjusted his gloves and walked round the front of the bonnet to get into the driving seat.

'Thank you,' said Sara, glancing sideways at the dark-suited figure.

'My pleasure,' said Ben Cavalli, laughing.

In spite of her tiredness, Sara slewed smartly round in her seat.

'You! What are you doing here?'

'Waiting for you to do up your safety belt. After that, I'm taking you home.'

'I'm not going anywhere with you,' announced Sara, fumbling for the door handle.

'It's locked,' he said with odious calm.

He reached across her, pulled the seat belt across her body and fastened it, with a crisp snap. Then he switched on the ignition, put the car in gear, and they pulled smoothly away from the kerb. Behind them, the revellers they had just left waved and blew kisses. Sara stared rigidly ahead of her.

'Let me out of this car.'

'Certainly. When we reach your apartment.'

She averted her face and watched the traffic, the familiar landmarks; the illuminated statue of Nelson on top of his column in Trafalgar Square; the government buildings of Whitehall, looking like a stage set for a Turkish ballet, seen through the trees of St James' Park. Ben did not disturb her reverie with conversation.

At last, they came to the apartment block where Sara rented a flat. It was a new acquisition. The address was known only to a few people and her number was not yet listed in the telephone book.

'How do you know where I live?' she demanded arctically.

'Sir Gerald.'

He swung the car into the forecourt and stopped in front of the glass door that led into the lobby. Sara could see the sleepy night porter peering at her from his cubbyhole.

'I see.' She undid the safety harness which snaked away into its hole with a near-silent swish. 'Thank you for bringing me home.'

He nodded, killed the engine, and got out. She had fully expected him to invite himself in, even to insist on accompanying her to her apartment. It was, she told herself furiously, a relief that he did nothing of the kind.

Sara let him help her out of the car, and then swept ahead, up the shallow steps and into the lobby. The inner door was locked, and the porter came forward to admit her.

'Goodnight,' she said to Ben over her shoulder, not turning to acknowledge his response or see him drive away.

She reached her top floor flat, almost running. Barely

pausing to close the door behind her, she flung herself on to the sofa and wept. She loved him so much. Even when he was cruel and teasing, even when, as now, he had looked at her as if she were an amusing object of no importance to him at all. Oh why, *why* had she had to fall in love with a man who had no use for her except to play a part in one of a succession of not very important affairs?

If only she had not let him make love to her, she thought, wrapping her arms round her shivering form, as her tears dried. It was all very well for Sir Gerald to say that now she was a tragic ballerina, but the price had been appalling. For her body would always remember. She might be strong-minded, she might put him out of her thoughts for hours at a time, but her body could always recall every touch.

How could he have such a profound effect on her and not be moved himself? Mopping her eyes on the corner of an already sopping handkerchief, Sara thought wryly that he probably did not begin to understand how she felt. If he did, he would be embarrassed.

As for his mother—well, obviously, she would much rather he was desperately in love with an available single girl than involved with his partner's wife, and, possibly, messy divorce. But Ben himself did not care for her, any more than Robert had done. He had not tried to contact her, or write to her, any more than Robert had done.

The only thing she could do, the only sensible thing, was to concentrate on her career and put her broken heart on one side. She passed a cold hand over her forehead. She must get some sleep. She was dancing again tomorrow night.

The doorbell rang, suddenly shrill, interrupting her reverie. She jumped and went to open it, expecting the porter. She must have dropped something in the hall. It couldn't be Ben. He couldn't get into the building without the porter ringing to check that it was all right. No, it couldn't be Ben.

Nevertheless she was enormously disappointed to see the porter peering at her over an enormous bunch of blue and white iris. Looking past him, she saw that the landing was full of flowers. She stared.

'Chap's brought the flowers round from the theatre,' Griggs told her cheerfully. 'You must have been a sensation, Miss Romana.'

'Er—thank you.'

Sara was bewildered. She had never received such an ovation and had no idea that the flowers that filled the stage after the performance became her personal responsibility to dispose of. She looked at the bank of flowers in some dismay.

'Better put them in water,' Griggs urged helpfully. Then his intercom buzzed and he shrugged. 'Someone else back late. I'll let them in. I'll send the rest of the flowers up then.'

She began to transfer the bouquets into the flat. When the lift arrived she barely looked up. The man who got out, however, with a large white box under one arm and a cane basket of roses in the other, was not the porter she expected.

She stopped as if she had been struck. 'Ben!' she said in a whisper.

'As you say,' he looked round in amusement. 'I hope you don't suffer from hay fever. Let's get this lot inside.'

Sara was familiar with his sense of humour but this, she felt, was no time for joking. She padded after him, aware of a feeling of breathless excitement, as if she were about to begin a dance instead of being at the end of an exhausting evening.

The competent Professor Cavalli stored all the flowers in her bath, put the long white box down carefully on the carpet, and took her in his arms. There was a long silence while Sara strove to keep her head and Ben did everything he could to make her lose it. Ben won.

'Now,' he said at last, still amused though his breath was coming rapidly and his eyes were not amused at all, 'you can stop being difficult and explain yourself. I take it that, contrary to the information you gave Gunilla, you are not marrying Robert Ericsson?' She nodded in bewilderment, and he inclined his head in acknowledgement, ticking the point off on his fingers.

'And, two, you have now permanently left Oxford. Where this,' he indicated the box, 'has been languishing unacknowledged for weeks.'

'Y-yes. But what is that?'

'The dress I was going to give you in Venice. Before you left. When I told you I loved you. I was going to send the boat away and lock you in your room. Only then I opened my mail. And it included the final reports that Mario had forwarded to me about a young ballet dancer I was supposed to be helping.' He went down on his knees beside her. 'Don't you see, my darling? That was the first time that I knew who you were. The previous papers had all called you Sara Romana. I had no idea. I'd no suspicion. And from that moment, my hands were tied.'

Sara shook her head. 'I don't understand.'

He stood up and turned away.

'You were, in some sort, my patient,' he said levelly. 'You needed treatment. Medical ethics are quite clear on the relationship between doctor and patient. I either had to send you to someone else—and Andrews was pretty clear that the clinic was your last hope—or treat you as a stranger. I couldn't do a damned thing until you were cured and out of my care.'

'I see,' Sara thought about that first, shattering occasion when she had come face to face with him in the Como clinic. He had looked so unmoved, so cold. 'I never thought of that,' she confessed now.

He looked over his shoulder, gravely questioning.

'Why didn't you tell me who you were? What had happened to you? I knew there was something wrong but you wouldn't let me get anywhere near you. Why were you so determined to keep me at a distance? You were, weren't you?'

Sara found she could not meet his eyes. At last, she nodded.

He came back to her side and hunkered down in front of her.

'Why?'

She swallowed. Her throat was dry and when she spoke it sounded as if her voice was scratching it. She swallowed again and said, 'I was afraid.'

Ben drew a sharp breath.

'Oh God. If only I'd known. I should have known. When I first saw you I should have guessed. They told me all about your case at the hospital.'

She looked up at that, startled. He gave a slightly twisted smile.

'Oh yes, your fame had gone before you, my darling. I was in Oxford to give a paper, and afterwards Andrews asked me back to his consulting rooms and talked about your injury. Not in detail, of course. But I knew you were a dancer. . . . What I didn't know—what nobody had the wit to tell me—was that you lived in the same house as young Franks.

'And I, of course, never thought I'd meet anyone other than undergraduates at that damned party.' He gave a crack of laughter. 'I nearly didn't go, do you know that? I'd got too much work to do. It was obvious that Andrews thought he ought to entertain me and because he couldn't, wished me on to young Franks. And then I wasn't sure how to get out of it without offending the boy. I didn't intend to stay long. I never thought I'd find you there.'

'Don't you usually expect to pick up girls at parties?' asked Sara with a touch of irony.

To her surprise, he flinched. 'Don't talk about it like that. You've always seemed ashamed of what happened that evening.'

'I'd never behaved like that before,' Sara told him honestly. 'I was ashamed. And surprised,' she added reflectively.

He trailed one long finger caressingly down her cheek.

'You're so young. I keep forgetting how young you are.'

'No younger than the other girls at that party,' Sara objected.

'In years, perhaps. But in experience—that's a different matter.'

'Well, I spent a lot of my adolescence working,' Sara told him defensively.

'I know.' He took her hands and held them hard between his own. 'Or rather, I know *now*. It was a material fact that I didn't know at the time. All I did know was that I couldn't let you go without at least trying to—to take it further. When I found you were a secretary, I was overjoyed.'

Sara regarded him narrowly. 'Why?'

'Because I needed a secretary. I'd already told old Fredericks I needed one. After I'd grilled young Franks and he told me where you worked, I rang Fredericks and said that he was to get you to agree to come to Venice, come hell or high water. He rather shook me by telling me that you'd go to Kathmandu if the money was right.'

Sara looked unhappy. 'I'm not mercenary,' she said with difficulty. 'It wasn't that. It was just that Mr Andrews kept talking about treatment all over the world and I simply hadn't got the money for it.'

Ben laughed softly. 'Again, I know that now. At the time—well, it had its advantages as well as its disadvantages. I offered you an enormous salary to make sure you came to Venice. I was a bit taken aback when you seemed as if you would come anyway. You hardly mentioned money. And you certainly weren't impressed by the amount I was offering.'

Sara was appalled. 'I'm sorry. Was it so huge? I didn't realise.'

'No, that was clear. What was pushing you out of Oxford, if it wasn't the money, then?'

Sara looked down at her hands folded between his own. Then she raised her eyes to his face. 'Robert,' she said in a whisper.

Ben's expression darkened. 'The intrusive fiancé, damn him. What had he done?'

She shrugged. 'Nothing, except turn up. I thought he was in America, you see. We—the engagement was broken after my accident and. . . .'

He interrupted her halting words. 'I know,' he said gently. 'Sir Gerald told me about him. Did he hurt you very badly, Sara?'

'At the time, yes,' she said steadily.

His hands tightened on hers.

'And now, he's hurt you again, you don't have to tell me. I know you're not engaged any more. I—asked.'

She stared at him in bewilderment. 'Of course we're not engaged. But Robert hasn't hurt me.'

Ben's eyes narrowed. 'He came to see you in Como. You left with him. Sir Gerald thought he was going to ask you to marry him. Didn't he?'

'Yes, he did,' she admitted, 'but I didn't think it would be a good idea. And I didn't leave with him.'

'Gunilla told me that you did.'

'Oh!' Sara was enlightened. She flushed slightly. 'That was just an excuse. It seemed too silly to say that I was running away from you. Which was the truth. So I said Robert was in a hurry. But actually he'd already gone.'

Ben releasd her hands and sank, cross-legged on to the carpet. His eyes never left her face and the beginnings of a smile dawned. Seeing the smile, Sara hurried on and told him all that Robert had said. His smile grew.

'So you're not feeling sad and jilted?'

Wide-eyed Sara shook her head. 'What gave you that idea?'

'Sir Gerald,' Ben told her succinctly. 'Sir Gerald's view is that you are now a great tragic ballerina. Which is a good thing. Because you have broken your heart over Robert Ericsson, which isn't.'

Sara snorted inelegantly.

'Robert! He's a spoilt child.'

'Oh quite.' Ben was smiling, but his eyes were watchful. 'But he still hurt you badly.'

She shrugged a dismissive shoulder. 'That was ages ago.' Her smile was a little twisted. 'And anyway, experience leads me to believe that I never really did quite break my heart over him.'

He did not miss the faint emphasis on the final pronoun. His eyes darkened.

'Then, who?'

She said, dully, 'You.'

He swore under his breath. Then he let her go and walked across to the French window. He had left the patio light on and stared out at her pots of spring flowers as if he was intending to paint them from memory.

'I can't ever make you forget that, can I?' Ben said in a low voice.

Not understanding him, she did not answer.

'Look, I know you may not believe this, but—I've never done anything like that before in my whole life. I thought you wanted me. I knew you were—wary. I was fairly certain that you'd been hurt before and were going carefully. But I was so certain that it was mutual, what I felt.' He slammed a fist against the window frame, making the whole plate of glass shake. 'That's male vanity, for you.'

Sara said bewildered, 'But surely. . . .'

'The trouble,' he went on, still refusing to look at her, 'is the damned world we live in. My students study virgins as if they were dinosaurs. And the people I know in Venice, my mother's cronies—well, they instil certain expectations. One imagines that everyone is as sophisticated as they are; as one is oneself.'

Sara flinched.

'So I never made allowances for the fact that you were a complete innocent. That what to me looked like——' he paused and his mouth thinned, 'passion, was no more than a sort of experimental attraction. There is no excuse for me, I can see that.'

Sara took a hasty step forward. 'No, there isn't,' she said furious. 'Experimental attraction, indeed. How dare you, Ben Cavalli? How *dare* you? What do you think I am—a schoolgirl with a crush on you?'

He flung himself round to confront her. 'Well?'

'I was in love with you, damn it,' she shouted at him, forgetting to be careful.

There was a frozen silence. Oh God, thought Sara, this is where he gives an embarrassed apology and retreats.

Ben, however, showed no signs of retreating. His eyes narrowed. The strong face was quite unreadable. He said unemotionally, 'You gave no indication of it. I think you must be imagining it.'

Sara shook her head sorrowfully. Now that she had revealed her most closely guarded secret, she felt that she had no pride or privacy left.

'No, I'm not. I didn't want to fall in love—with anyone. Particularly not with you.

The hooded eyes sparked.

'Why particularly not me?' he asked smoothly.

She gave a wry smile. 'You must know yourself. You were out of my league. And—anyway—they kept telling me that you were going to marry soon. It was clear that I could only be an interlude.' She shivered. 'And I knew that I couldn't handle that. Not then.'

Nor am I sure I can handle it now, she thought, but she did not say that. Or not out loud.

'I obviously did not matter to you. I hardly ever saw you. When I did, we fought. And then I left and you did nothing about it.'

He smiled. 'When you left, you went straight into the care of the kindest people in Venice. I knew that I had to keep my distance, if you were to be my patient, but I wasn't letting you out in the world unprotected. Salvatore had strict instructions to make sure you were safe and comfortable and report back to me regularly. Which he did.'

'You take your responsibilities seriously,' she said, a shadow behind her smile.

'Responsibilities?' Ben gave a harsh laugh. 'You should ask Salvatore if he thought I was looking after my responsibilities. He thought I was out of my mind. All the servants did. I kept asking them about you, watching you grilling Uncle Luigi. Yes,' he added reflectively, 'I was even jealous of him. You clearly adored him and you didn't even like me.'

'*Like* you?' She drew a long breath. 'Like you?' she hissed, ignoring caution in her indignation. 'I fell for you from the first moment you accosted me on the stairs, and I never got my balance back.'

Almost as if he were talking to himself, he said, 'I don't believe it.'

'Oh, I did everything I could to fight it,' Sara acknowledged proudly. 'I didn't admit it to myself for weeks. I tried to hide it from you. But when, the night of the fog, everything happened so quickly, I just stopped trying.'

He took an eager step forward. Sara glared at him.

'So you can stop thinking that you did something unforgivable to me. You didn't do a thing to me. *We* made love. *I* participated.'

She stopped, her breast heaving with righteous anger.

'You did indeed,' agreed Ben, his eyes alight with affectionate laughter. 'Come here.'

In spite of her anger, she allowed him to take her into a hard embrace. At last, she turned her head against his shoulder, and surreptitiously blinked a tear from the corner of her eye. She had little doubt that they would end in bed tonight and, though it would be heaven for as long as he wanted her, she knew even now that she would be devastated when he left. But she must hide that from him at all costs.

He stroked her hair with a hand that shook slightly.

'But my darling, why did you cry so desperately, that night? I wanted to stay with you. I was shocked, shaken, but I wanted to take care of you. Only you sent me away. You weren't pretending anything then. You wanted me out of the room.'

'Yes,' Sara agreed in a muffled tone. She turned her lips against his neck.

'Why?' he persisted, though she felt with a thrill the little shiver that convulsed him at her touch.

She hesitated. Then, flatly, she said. 'Because, however much in love I might have been, you didn't—and don't—love me.'

There was absolute silence. The hand on her hair stilled. For a moment, it seemed almost as if he had stopped breathing. Ben said in a strangled voice, 'Say that again.'

'You don't love me,' Sara muttered.

'Are,' he demanded, 'you out of your mind?'

She turned to look up at him, green eyes shadowed.

'No,' Ben shook his head in wonderment. 'You believe it. You really believe that rubbish.'

He held her away from him and began to speak very slowly and carefully.

'I was so much in love with you that I wouldn't leave you. I wasn't supposed to stay at the Palazzo, you know. I should have delivered you into Uncle Luigi's hands and then gone straight up to Como to relieve poor old Mario. Daniella kept visiting to point that out.'

'Oh?' Sara's eyebrows rose. 'I didn't get that impression.'

'I know exactly what impression you got, little cat,' Ben said appreciatively. 'My mother told me and I thought she must be mistaken, but I see she wasn't. My interest in Daniella is nil and always has been. Mario, on the other hand, is an old friend of the family. Daniella, when bored, can be—let us say—something of an embarrassment. She gets very bored when Mario is in Como for a long stretch at a time. She could go up there, of course, and live with him, but it is too quiet for her. So, since I was the reason that her husband was not with her in Venice taking her to the parties and nightclubs she had been invited to, I was honour-bound to escort her myself. It was,' he added with feeling, 'a damned nuisance. And if I hadn't been madly in love with you, I wouldn't have put up with it for a minute. But I couldn't leave you behind.'

Sara was impressed. She was still fairly certain that Daniella's object had been to lure Ben into an affair, but there was no doubt of the distaste in his voice when he spoke of her. Sara looked down at the hand that held hers. Very slowly, he brought her fingers to his lips.

'Sara,' Ben said huskily. 'Darling Sara. I loved you so much. You were so sweet—and kind to Uncle Luigi—and funny—and brave. You spat like a wildcat every time you thought your privacy was about to be invaded. But when you forgot to defend yourself——' He turned her hand over and held the palm against his lips. 'I promised myself I'd get you to confide in me, drop your defences. But you never did.'

'I was too frightened,' Sara admitted honestly.

His jaw tautened. 'That was my fault.'

'No,' she protested, cupping his face in her slender hands and turning honest eyes to meet his. 'I was—afraid of feeling, any sort of feeling. I had relied on Robert, you see, and he had let me down badly. It seemed that feeling was something you could only afford when you were on top of the world. And I wasn't. I didn't know whether I had any career. I didn't know what I was going to do after I left Venice. I was frightened all the time. But never of you. Only—of what I felt for you.'

'Darling,' he hugged her. 'Are you still frightened?'

Sara thought. She was apprehensive, exhilarated, but frightened?

'No,' she said, with absolute conviction.

He let out a long, relieved breath.

'Thank God for that. Then we'll get married next week.'

She jumped. 'Married?'

The blue eyes were brilliant with amusement. 'I don't know whether your intentions were dishonourable, Miss Romana, but I am only prepared to settle for legal matrimony,' Ben told her firmly.

'But——'

'Legal,' he insisted, 'and binding. I'm not letting you out of my sight ever again, except when you dance. I can't live without you, and I don't intend to try. We'll get married as soon as I can arrange it.'

Overwhelmed by this masterful disposal of her future, Sara nevertheless saw a difficulty. 'You mean that you're going to do the honourable thing?' she asked in a dissatisfied voice.

His eyes narrowed. 'You have some objection to marriage?' he asked haughtily. 'There is an alternative you would prefer?'

'Oh no. No, I'd love to marry you,' Sara said hurriedly. 'It's just that. . . .'

'Well?' Ben was still frowning, but the sapphire eyes belied his grim expression. Sara could feel an answering smile beginning to curl her own lips.

'Well, next week is such a long time,' she pointed out demurely, 'for you to keep on being honourable,' she explained.

'On the contrary,' Ben was dulcet. 'I intend to start as I mean to go on. I promised I'd look after you, didn't I? I'm not going to leave you here all alone, all night, with this mountain of flowers. Who knows what might be concealed in them?'

'Oh, quite,' said Sara, beginning to enjoy herself. She reached for his hand, and found hers warmly clasped, their fingers twining.

'Rattlesnakes,' said Ben, watching her mouth 'Aren't you tired? Don't you need to go to bed? Which is your room?'

'That one,' said Sara, leading him to it. 'And I don't think there'll be any rattlesnakes.'

'Black widow spiders,' Ben assured her, opening the door and drawing her after him into the warm darkness. His arms slid round her under her jacket. Sara began to tremble convulsively.

'Black widows come in bunches of bananas, don't they?' she objected, trying to maintain the tone of the conversation.

'Mmm,' He was kissing her neck under her hair, withdrawing hairpins until it fell and floated about her shoulders. 'Don't be difficult. How do you know there isn't a bunch of bananas tucked away in that jungle in the bath?'

Sara succumbed to delight. 'I don't. I'm sure there

may be. Probably is. I need to be looked after. Stay with me, Ben.'

He strained her against him, and she could hear his heart racing under his ribs. Lovingly, and with absolute confidence, she began to touch him, returning caress for caress in utter abandon.

'For ever!' Ben whispered, as they fell, enmeshed in their growing need, among the cushions and pillows. 'And this time,' he said, against her temple, 'I'm not going to let you send me away. Not ever again. We'll be together from now onwards, and if you want to argue about it, I'll. . . .'

'Yes?' murmured Sara, kissing his shoulder.

'Convince you,' said Ben on a shaken laugh. 'Like this.'

And proceeded to demonstrate.